This book belongs to:

_____

_____

An Illustrated Treasury of
READ-ALOUD CLASSICS
for Young People

An Illustrated Treasury of
READ-ALOUD CLASSICS
for Young People

Ten-Minute Selections from the World's Best-Loved
Books for Parent and Child to Share

BLACK DOG
& LEVENTHAL
PUBLISHERS
NEW YORK

Published by
Black Dog & Leventhal Publishers, Inc.
151 West 19th Street
New York, NY 10011

Distributed by
Workman Publishing Company
708 Broadway
New York, NY 10003

Page 222 represents a continuation of this copyright page.

Manufactured in Singapore

Cover and interior design by Liz Driesbach

Cover illustration by Jessie Willcox Smith

ISBN: 1-57912-288-4

h g f e d c b a

Library of Congress Cataloging-in-Publication Data available on file.

Contents

Homer Price goes to visit his uncle Ulysses at his lunchroom in Centerburg. Uncle Ulysses needs some help with his automatic doughnut machine. He asks Homer to give him a hand with it and to mix up a batch of doughnut batter. After Homer puts the machine together, he makes a lot of doughnuts!

Homer Price

ROBERT McCLOSKEY

CHAPTER 3
THE DOUGHNUTS

One Friday night in November, Homer overheard his mother talking on the telephone to Aunt Agnes over in Centerburg. "I'll stop by with the car in about half an hour and we can go to the meeting together," she said, because tonight was the night the Ladies' Club was meeting to discuss plans for a box social and to knit and sew for the Red Cross.

"I think I'll come along and keep Uncle Ulysses company while you and Aunt Agnes are at the meeting," said Homer.

So after Homer had combed his hair and his mother had looked to see if she had her knitting instructions and the right size needles, they started for town.

Homer's Uncle Ulysses and Aunt Agnes have a very up-and-coming lunchroom over in Centerburg, just across from the courthouse on the town square. Uncle Ulysses is a man with advanced ideas and a weakness for labor-saving devices. He equipped the lunchroom with automatic toasters, an automatic coffee-maker, an automatic

dishwasher, and an automatic doughnut-maker. All just the latest thing in labor-saving devices. Aunt Agnes would throw up her hands and sigh every time Uncle Ulysses bought a new labor-saving device. Sometimes she became unkindly disposed toward him for days and days. She was of the opinion that Uncle Ulysses just frittered away his spare time over at the barber shop with the sheriff and the boys, so what was the good of a labor-saving device that gave you more time to fritter?

When Homer and his mother got to Centerburg they stopped at the lunchroom, and after Aunt Agnes had come out and said, "My, how that boy does grow!" which was what she always said, she went off with Homer's mother in the car. Homer went into the lunchroom and said, "Howdy, Uncle Ulysses!"

"Oh, hello, Homer. You're just in time," said Uncle Ulysses. "I've been going over this automatic doughnut machine, oiling the machinery and cleaning the works . . . wonderful things, these labor-saving devices."

"Opfwo-oof!!" sighed Uncle Ulysses and, "Look here, Homer, you've got a mechanical mind. See if you can find where these two pieces fit in. I'm going across to the barber shop for a spell, 'cause there's somethin' I've got to talk to the sheriff about. There won't be much business here until the double feature is over, and I'll be back before then."

Then as Uncle Ulysses went out the door he said, "Uh, Homer, after you get the pieces in place, would you mind mixing up a batch of doughnut batter and putting it in the machine? You could turn the switch and make a few doughnuts to have on hand for the crowd after the movie . . . if you don't mind."

"O.K." said Homer, "I'll take care of everything."

A few minutes later a customer came in and said, "Good evening, Bud."

Homer looked up from putting the last piece in the doughnut machine and said, "Good evening, sir, what can I do for you?"

"Well, young feller, I'd like a cup o' coffee and some doughnuts," said the customer.

"I'm sorry, mister, but we won't have any doughnuts for about half an hour, until I can mix some dough and start this machine. I could give you some very fine sugar rolls instead."

"Well, Bud, I'm in no real hurry so I'll just have a cup o' coffee and wait around a bit for the doughnuts. Fresh doughnuts are always worth waiting for is what I always say."

"O.K." said Homer, and he drew a cup of coffee from Uncle Ulysses' super automatic coffeemaker.

"Nice place you've got here," said the customer.

"Oh, yes," replied Homer, "this is a very up-and-coming lunchroom with all the latest improvements."

"Yes," said the stranger, "must be a good business. I'm in business too. A traveling man in outdoor advertising. I'm a sandwich man, Mr. Gabby's my name."

"My name is Homer. I'm glad to meet you, Mr. Gabby. It must be a fine profession, traveling and advertising sandwiches."

"Oh no," said Mr. Gabby, "I don't advertise sandwiches, I just wear any kind of an ad, one sign on front and one sign on behind, this way . . . like a sandwich. Ya know what I mean?"

"Oh, I see. That must be fun, and you travel too?" asked Homer as he got out the flour and the baking powder.

"Yeah, I ride the rods between jobs, on freight trains, ya know what I mean?"

"Yes, but isn't that dangerous?" asked Homer.

"Of course there's a certain amount a risk, but you take any method a travel these days, it's all dangerous. Ya know what I mean? Now take airplanes for instance . . ."

Just then a large, shiny, black car stopped in front of the lunchroom and a chauffeur helped a lady out of the rear door. They both came inside and the lady smiled at Homer and said, "We've stopped for a light snack. Some doughnuts and coffee would be simply marvelous."

Then Homer said, "I'm sorry, ma'am, but the doughnuts won't be ready until I make this batter and start Uncle Ulysses' doughnut machine."

"Well now aren't you a clever young man to know how to make doughnuts!"

"Well," blushed Homer, "I've really never done it before but I've got a recipe to follow."

"Now, young man, you simply must allow me to help. You know, I haven't made doughnuts for years, but I know the best recipe for doughnuts. It's marvelous, and we really must use it."

"But, Ma'am . . ." said Homer.

"Now just wait till you taste these doughnuts," said the lady. "Do you have an apron?" she asked, as she took off her fur coat and her rings and her jewelry and rolled up her sleeves. "Charles," she said to the chauffeur, "hand me that baking powder, that's right, and, young man, we'll need some nutmeg."

So Homer and the chauffeur stood by and handed things and cracked the eggs while the lady mixed and stirred. Mr. Gabby sat on his stool, sipped his coffee, and looked on with great interest.

"There!" said the lady when all of the ingredients were mixed. "Just wait till you taste these doughnuts!"

"It looks like an awful lot of batter," said Homer as he stood on a chair and poured the batter into the doughnut machine with the help of the chauffeur. "It's about ten times as much as Uncle Ulysses ever makes."

"But wait till you taste them!" said the lady with an eager look and a smile.

Homer got down from the chair and pushed a button on the machine marked "Start." Rings of batter started dropping into the hot fat. After a ring of batter was cooked on one side an automatic gadget turned it over and the other side would cook. Then another automatic gadget gave the doughnut a little push and it rolled neatly down a little chute, all ready to eat.

"That's a simply fascinating machine," said the lady as she waited for the first doughnut to roll out.

"Here, young man, you must have the first one. Now isn't that just too delicious!? Isn't it simply marvelous?"

"Yes, Ma'am, it's very good," replied Homer as the lady handed doughnuts to Charles and to Mr. Gabby and asked if they didn't think they were simply divine doughnuts.

"It's an old family recipe!" said the lady with pride.

Homer poured some coffee for the lady and her chauffeur and for Mr. Gabby, and a glass of milk for himself. Then they all sat down at the lunch counter to enjoy another few doughnuts apiece.

"I'm so glad you enjoy my doughnuts," said the lady. "But now, Charles, we really must be going. If you will just take this apron, Homer, and put two dozen doughnuts in a bag to take to the young man." She rolled down her sleeves and put on her jewelry, then Charles managed to get her into her big fur coat.

"Good night, young man, I haven't had so much fun in years. I really haven't!" said the lady as she went out the door and into the big shiny car.

"You bet!" said Homer. Then he and Mr. Gabby stood and watched the automatic doughnut machine make doughnuts.

After a few dozen more doughnuts had rolled down the little chute, Homer said, "I guess that's about enough doughnuts to sell to the after-theater customers. I'd better turn the machine off for awhile."

Homer pushed the button marked "Stop" and there was a little click, but nothing happened. The rings of batter kept right on dropping into the hot fat, and an automatic gadget kept right on turning them over, and another automatic gadget kept right on giving them a little push, and the doughnuts kept right on rolling down the little chute, all ready to eat.

"That's funny," said Homer, "I'm sure that's the right button!" He pushed it again but the automatic doughnut maker kept right on making doughnuts. "Well I guess I must have put one of those pieces in backward," said Homer.

"Then it might stop if you pushed the button marked 'Start,'" said Mr. Gabby.

Homer did, and the doughnuts still kept rolling down the little chute, just as regular as a clock can tick.

"I guess we could sell a few more doughnuts," said Homer, "but I'd better telephone Uncle Ulysses over at the barber shop." Homer gave the number and while he waited for someone to answer he counted thirty-seven doughnuts roll down the little chute.

Finally someone answered, "Hello! This is the sarber bhop, I mean the barber shop."

"Oh, hello, Sheriff. This is Homer. Could I speak to Uncle Ulysses?"

"Well, he's playing pinochle right now," said the sheriff. "Anythin' I can tell 'im?"

"Yes," said Homer. "I pushed the button marked 'Stop' on the doughnut machine but the rings of batter keep right on dropping into the hot fat, and an automatic gadget keeps right on turning them over, and another automatic gadget keeps giving them a little push, and the doughnuts keep right on rolling down the little chute! It won't stop!"

"O.K. wold the hire, I mean, hold the wire and I'll tell 'im." Then Homer looked over his shoulder and counted another twenty-one doughnuts roll down the little chute, all ready to eat. Then the sheriff said, "He'll be right over. . . . Just gotta finish this hand."

"That's good," said Homer. "G'by, Sheriff."

The window was full of doughnuts by now so Homer and Mr. Gabby had to hustle around and start stacking them on plates and trays and lining them up on the counter.

"Sure are a lot of doughnuts!" said Homer.

"You bet!" said Mr. Gabby. I lost count at 1,202 and that was quite a while back."

People had begun to gather outside the lunchroom window, and someone was saying, "There are almost as many doughnuts as there are people in Centerburg, and I wonder how in tarnation Ulysses thinks he can sell all of 'em!"

Every once in awhile somebody would come inside and buy some, but while somebody bought two to eat and a dozen to take home, the machine made three dozen more.

By the time Uncle Ulysses and the sheriff arrived and pushed through the crowd, the lunchroom was a calamity of doughnuts! Doughnuts in the window, doughnuts piled high on the shelves, doughnuts stacked on the plates, doughnuts lined up twelve deep all along the counter, and doughnuts still rolling down the little chute, just as regular as a clock can tick.

"Hello, Sheriff, hello, Uncle Ulysses, we're having a little trouble here," said Homer.

"Well, I'll be dunked!!" said Uncle Ulysses.

"Dernd ef you won't be when Aggy gits home," said the sheriff.

"Mighty fine doughnuts though. What'll you do with 'em all, Ulysses?"

Uncle Ulysses groaned and said, "What will Aggy say? We'll never sell 'em all."

Then Mr. Gabby, who hadn't said anything for a long time, stopped piling doughnuts and said, "What you need is an advertising man. Ya know what I mean? You got the doughnuts, ya gotta create a market. . . . Understand? . . . It's balancing the demand with the supply . . . that sort of thing."

"Yep!" said Homer. "Mr. Gabby's right. We have to enlarge our market. He's an advertising sandwich man, so if we hire him, he can walk up and down in front of the theater and get the customers."

"You're hired, Mr. Gabby!" said Uncle Ulysses. Then everybody pitched in to paint the signs and to get Mr. Gabby sandwiched between. They painted "SALE ON DOUGH-NUTS" in big letters on the window too.

Meg Murry and her younger brother, Charles Wallace, desperately miss their scientist father, who has mysteriously disappeared. The mystery, however, slowly unravels when they meet three peculiar women— one constantly quotes famous people, another speaks in vibrations— who tell them that "there is such a thing as a tesseract," or a wrinkle in time! The two children and Meg's schoolmate, Calvin, are whisked away by these outlandish strangers, named Mrs. Whatsit, Mrs. Who, and Mrs. Which, to a new place, or dimension, where they begin their valiant rescue of their father.

A Wrinkle in Time

MADELEINE L'ENGLE

CHAPTER 4
THE BLACK THING

The trees were lashed into a violent frenzy. Meg screamed and clutched at Calvin, and Mrs. Which's authoritative voice called out, "Qquiett, chilldd!"

Did a shadow fall across the moon or did the moon simply go out, extinguished as abruptly and completely as a candle? There was still the sound of leaves, a terrified, terrifying rushing. All light was gone. Darkness was complete. Suddenly the wind was gone, and all sound. Meg felt that Calvin was being torn from her. When she reached for him her fingers touched nothing.

She screamed out, "Charles!" and whether it was to help him or for him to help her, she did not know. The word was flung back down her throat and she choked on it.

She was completely alone.

She had lost the protection of Calvin's hand. Charles was nowhere, either to save or to turn to. She was alone in a fragment of nothingness. No light, no sound, no feeling. Where was her body? She tried to move in her panic, but there was nothing to move. Just as light and sound had vanished, she was gone, too. The corporeal Meg simply was not.

Then she felt her limbs again. Her legs and arms were tingling faintly, as though they had been asleep. She blinked her eyes rapidly, but though she herself was somehow back, nothing else was. It was not as simple as darkness, or absence of light. Darkness has a tangible quality; it can be moved through and felt; in darkness you can bark your shins; the world of things still exists around you. She was lost in a horrifying void.

It was the same way with the silence. This was more than silence. A deaf person can feel vibrations. Here there was nothing to feel.

Suddenly she was aware of her heart beating rapidly within the cage of her ribs. Had it stopped before? What had made it start again? The tingling in her arms and legs grew stronger, and suddenly she felt movement. This movement, she felt, must be the turning of the Earth, rotating on its axis, traveling its elliptic course about the Sun. And this feeling of moving with the earth was somewhat like the feeling of being in the ocean, out in the ocean beyond this rising and falling of the breakers, lying on the moving water, pulsing gently with the swells, and feeling the gentle, inexorable tug of the Moon.

I am asleep; I am dreaming, she thought. I'm having a nightmare. I want to wake up. Let me wake up.

"Well!" Charles Wallace's voice said. "That was quite a trip! I do think you might have warned us."

Light began to pulse and quiver. Meg blinked and shoved shakily at her glasses and there was Charles Wallace standing indignantly in front of her, his hands on his hips. "Meg!" he shouted. "Calvin! Where are you?"

She saw Charles, she heard him, but she could not go to him. She could not shove through the strange, trembling light to meet him.

Calvin's voice came as though it were pushing through a cloud. "Well, just give me time, will you? I'm older than you are."

Meg gasped. It wasn't that Calvin wasn't there and then that he was. It wasn't that part of him came first and then the rest of him followed, like a hand and then an arm, an eye and then a nose. It was a sort of shimmering, a looking at Calvin through water, through smoke, through fire, and then there he was, solid and reassuring.

"Meg!" Charles Wallace's voice came. "Meg! Calvin, where's Meg?"

"I'm right here," she tried to say, but her voice seemed to be caught at its source.

"Meg!" Calvin cried, and he turned around, looking about wildly.

"Mrs. Which, you haven't left Meg behind, have you?" Charles Wallace shouted.

"If you've hurt Meg, any of you—" Calvin started, but suddenly Meg felt a violent thrust through a wall of glass.

"Oh, there you are!" Charles Wallace said, and rushed over to her and hugged her.

"But where am I?" Meg asked breathlessly, relieved to hear that her voice was now coming out of her in more or less a normal way.

She looked around rather wildly. They were standing in a sunlit field, and the air about them was moving with the delicious fragrance that comes only on the rarest of spring days when the sun's touch is gentle and the apple blossoms are just beginning to unfold. She pushed her glasses up on her nose to reassure herself that what she was seeing was real.

They had left the silver glint of a biting autumn evening; and now around them everything was golden with light. The grasses of the field were a tender new green, and scattered about were tiny, multicolored flowers. Meg turned slowly to face a mountain reaching so high into the sky that its peak was lost in a crown of puffy white clouds. From the trees at the base of the mountain came a sudden singing of birds. There was an air of such ineffable peace and joy all around her that her heart's wild thumping slowed.

"When shall we three meet again,
In thunder, lightning, or in rain,"

came Mrs. Who's voice. Suddenly the three of them were there, Mrs. Whatsit with her pink stole askew; Mrs. Who with her spectacles gleaming; and Mrs. Which still little more than a shimmer. Delicate, multicolored butterflies were fluttering about them, as though in greeting.

Mrs. Whatsit and Mrs. Who began to giggle, and they giggled until it seemed that, whatever their private joke was, they would fall down laughing, too. It became vaguely darker and more solid; and then there appeared a figure in a black robe and a black peaked hat, beady eyes, a beaked nose, and long gray hair; one bony claw clutched a broomstick.

"Wwell, jusstt ttoo kkeepp yyou girrlls happpy," the strange voice said, and Mrs. Whatsit and Mrs. Who fell into each other's arms in gales of laughter.

"If you ladies have had your fun I think you should tell Calvin and Meg a little more about all this," Charles Wallace said coldly. "You scared Meg half out of her wits, whisking her off this way without any warning."

"*Finxerunt animi, raro et perpauca loquentis*," Mrs. Who intoned. "Horace. To action little, less to words inclined."

"Mrs. Who, I wish you'd stop quoting!" Charles Wallace sounded very annoyed.

Mrs. Whatsit adjusted her stole. "But she finds it so difficult to verbalize, Charles dear. It helps her if she can quote instead of working out words of her own."

"Anndd wee mussttn'tt looose ourr sensses of hummorr," Mrs. Which said. "Thee onnlly wway ttoo ccope withh ssometthingg ddeadly sseriouss iss tto ttry ttoo trreatt itt a llittle lligghtly."

"But that's going to be hard for Meg," Mrs. Whatsit said. "It's going to be hard for her to realize that we are serious."

"What about me?" Calvin asked.

"The life of your father isn't at stake," Mrs. Whatsit told him.

"What about Charles Wallace, then?"

Mrs. Whatsit's unoiled-door-hinge voice was warm with affection and pride. "Charles Wallace knows. Charles Wallace knows that it's far more than just the life of his father. Charles Wallace knows what's at stake."

"But remember," Mrs. Who said, "Nothing is hopeless; we must hope for everything."

"Where are we now, and how did we get here?" Calvin asked.

"Uriel, the third planet of the star Malak in the spiral nebula Messier 101."

"This I'm supposed to believe?" Calvin asked indignantly.

"Aas yyou llike," Mrs. Which said coldly.

For some reason Meg felt that Mrs. Which, despite her looks and ephemeral broomstick, was someone in whom one could put complete trust. "It doesn't seem any more peculiar than anything else that's happened."

"Well, then, someone just tell me how we got here!" Calvin's voice was still angry and his freckles seemed to stand out on his face. "Even traveling at the speed of light it would take us years and years to get here."

"Oh, we don't travel at the speed of anything," Mrs. Whatsit explained earnestly. "We tesser. Or you might say, we wrinkle."

"Clear as mud," Calvin said.

Tesser, Meg thought. Could that have anything to do with Mother's tesseract?

She was about to ask when Mrs. Which started to speak, and one did not interrupt when Mrs. Which was speaking. "Mrs. Whatsit iss yyoungg andd nnaive."

"She keeps thinking she can explain things in words," Mrs. Who said. "*Qui plus sait, plus se tait*. French, you know. The more a man knows, the less he talks."

"But she has to use words for Meg and Calvin," Charles reminded Mrs. Who. "If you brought them along, they have a right to know what's going on."

Meg went up to Mrs. Which. In the intensity of her question she had forgotten all about the tesseract. "Is my father here?"

Mrs. Which shook her head. "Nnott heeere, Megg. Llet Mrs. Which expllainn. Shee isss yyoungg annd thee llanguage of worrds iss eeasierr fforr hherr thann itt iss ffor Mrs. Whoo andd mee."

"We stopped here," Mrs. Whatsit explained, "more or less to catch our breath. And to give you a chance to know what you're up against."

"But what about Father?" Meg asked. "Is he all right?"

"For the moment, love, yes. He's one of the reasons we're here. But you see, he's only one."

"Well, where is he? Please take me to him!"

"We can't, not yet," Charles said. "You have to be patient, Meg."

"But I'm not patient!" Meg cried passionately. "I've never been patient!"

Mrs. Who's glasses shone at her gently. "If you want to help your father then you must learn patience. *Vitam impendere vero*. To stake one's life for the truth. That is what we must do."

"That is what your father is doing." Mrs. Whatsit nodded, her voice, like Mrs. Who's, very serious, very solemn. Then she smiled her radiant smile. "Now! Why don't you three children wander around and Charles can explain things a little. You're perfectly safe on Uriel. That's why we stopped here to rest."

"But aren't you coming with us?" Meg asked fearfully.

There was silence for a moment. Then Mrs. Which raised her authoritative hand. "Sshoww themm," she said to Mrs. Whatsit, and at something in her voice Meg felt prickles of apprehension.

"Now?" Mrs. Whatsit asked, her creaky voice rising to a squeak. Whatever it was Mrs. Which wanted them to see, it was something that made Mrs. Whatsit uncomfortable, too.

"Nnoww," Mrs. Which said. "Tthey mmay aas welll knoww."

"Should—should I change?" Mrs. Whatsit asked.

"Bbetter."

"I hope it won't upset the children too much," Mrs. Whatsit murmured, as though to herself.

"Should I change, too?" Mrs. Who asked. "Oh, but I've had fun in these clothes. But I'll have to admit Mrs. Whatsit is the best at it. *Das Werk lobt den Meister*. German. The work proves the craftsman. Shall I transform now, too?"

Mrs. Which shook her head. "Nnott yett. Nnott heere. Yyou mmay wwaitt."

"Now, don't be frightened, loves," Mrs. Whatsit said. Her plump little body began to shimmer, to quiver, to shift. The wild colors of her clothes became muted, whitened. The pudding-bag shape stretched, lengthened, merged. And suddenly before the children was a creature more beautiful than any Meg had even imagined, and the beauty lay in far more than the outward description. Outwardly Mrs. Whatsit was surely no longer a Mrs. Whatsit. She was a marble white body with powerful flanks, something like a horse but at the same time completely unlike a horse, for from the magnificently modeled back sprang a nobly formed torso, arms, and a head resembling a man's, but a man with a perfection of dignity and virtue, and exaltation of joy such as Meg had never before seen. No, she thought, it's not like a Greek centaur. Not in the least.

From the shoulders slowly a pair of wings unfolded, wings made of rainbows, of light upon water, of poetry.

Calvin fell to his knees.

Charlie Bucket has won a ticket to visit Willy Wonka's famous chocolate factory. Only five children are allowed inside. Violet Beauregarde is one of them. She decides to sample one of Wonka's inventions during the tour of his factory—but she doesn't count on the amazing consequences. All the children and their parents, learn a lesson about greed—and bad habits—from Willy and his assistants, the Oompa-Loompas.

Charlie and the Chocolate Factory

ROALD DAHL

CHAPTER 21
GOOD-BYE, VIOLET

My dear sir!" cried Mr. Wonka, "when I start selling this gum in the shops it will change everything! It will be the end of all kitchens and all cooking! There will be no more marketing to do! No more buying of meat and groceries! There will be no knives and forks at mealtimes! No plates! No washing up! No garbage! No mess! Just a little strip of Wonka's magic chewing gum—and that's all you'll ever need at breakfast, lunch, and supper! This piece of gum I've just made happens to be tomato soup, roast beef, and blueberry pie, but you can have almost anything you want!"

"What do you mean, it's tomato soup, roast beef, and blueberry pie?" said Violet Beauregarde.

"If you were to start chewing it," said Mr. Wonka, "then that is exactly what you would get on the menu. It's absolutely amazing! You can actually feel the food going down your throat and into your tummy! And you can taste it perfectly! And it fills you up! It satisfies you! It's terrific!"

"It's utterly impossible," said Veruca Salt.

"Just so long as it's gum," shouted Violet Beauregarde, "just so long as it's a piece of gum and I can chew it, then that's for me!" And quickly she took her own world-record piece of chewing gum out of her mouth and stuck it behind her left ear. "Come on, Mr. Wonka," she said, "hand over this magic gum of yours and we'll see if the thing works."

"Now, Violet," said Mrs. Beauregarde, her mother; "don't let's do anything silly, Violet."

"I want the gum!" Violet said obstinately. "What's so silly?"

"I would rather you didn't take it," Mr. Wonka told her gently. "You see, I haven't got it quite right yet. There are still one or two things . . ."

"Oh, to heck with that!" said Violet, and suddenly, before Mr. Wonka could stop her, she shot out a fat hand and grabbed the stick of gum out of the little drawer and popped it in her mouth. At once, her huge well-trained jaws started chewing away on it like a pair of tongs.

"Don't!" said Mr. Wonka.

"Fabulous!" shouted Violet. "It's tomato soup! It's hot and creamy and delicious! I can feel it running down my throat!"

"Stop!" said Mr. Wonka. "The gum isn't ready yet! It's not right!"

"Of course it's right!" said Violet. "It's working beautifully! Oh my, what lovely soup this is!"

"Spit it out!" said Mr. Wonka.

"It's changing!" shouted Violet, chewing and grinning both at the same time. "The second course is coming up! It's roast beef! It's tender and juicy! Oh boy, what a flavor! The baked potato is marvelous, too! It's got a crispy skin and it's all filled with butter inside!"

"But how in-teresting, Violet," said Mrs. Beauregarde. "You are a clever girl."

"Keep chewing, kiddo!" said Mr. Beauregarde. "Keep right on chewing, baby! This is a great day for the Beauregardes! Our little girl is the first person in the world to have a chewing-gum meal!"

Everybody was watching Violet Beauregarde as she stood there chewing this extraordinary gum. Little Charlie Bucket was staring at her absolutely spellbound, watching her huge rubbery lips as they pressed and unpressed with the chewing, and Grandpa Joe stood beside him, gaping at the girl. Mr. Wonka was wringing his hands and saying, "No, no, no, no, no! It isn't ready for eating! It isn't right! You mustn't do it!"

"Blueberry pie and cream!" shouted Violet. "Here it comes! Oh my, it's perfect! It's beautiful! It's . . . it's exactly as though I'm swallowing it! It's as though I'm chewing and swallowing great big spoonfuls of the most marvelous blueberry pie in the world!"

"Good heavens, girl," shrieked Mrs. Beauregarde suddenly, staring at Violet, "what's happening to your nose!"

"Oh, be quiet, mother, and let me finish!" said Violet.

"It's turning blue!" screamed Mrs. Beauregarde. "Your nose is turning blue as a blueberry!"

"Your mother is right!" shouted Mr. Beauregarde. "Your whole nose has gone purple!"

"What do you mean?" said Violet, still chewing away.

"Your cheeks!" screamed Mrs. Beauregarde. "They're turning blue as well! So is your chin! Your whole face is turning blue!"

"Spit that gum out at once!" ordered Mr. Beauregarde.

"Mercy! Save us!" yelled Mrs. Beauregarde. "The girl's going blue and purple all over! Even her hair is changing color! Violet, you're turning violet, Violet! What is happening to you!"

"I told you I hadn't got it quite right," sighed Mr. Wonka, shaking his head sadly.

"I'll say you haven't!" cried Mrs. Beauregarde. "Just look at the girl now!"

Everybody was staring at Violet. And what a terrible peculiar sight she was! Her face and hands and legs and neck, in fact the skin all over her body, as well as her great big mop of curly hair, had turned a brilliant, purplish-blue, the color of blueberry juice!

"It always goes wrong when we come to the dessert," sighed Mr. Wonka. "It's the blueberry pie that does it. But I'll get it right one day, you wait and see."

"Violet," screamed Mrs. Beauregarde again, "you're swelling up!"

"I feel sick," Violet said.

"You're swelling up!" screamed Mrs. Beauregarde again.

"I feel most peculiar!" gasped Violet.

"I'm not surprised!" said Mr. Beauregarde.

"Great heavens, girl!" screeched Mrs. Beauregarde. "You're blowing up like a balloon!"

"Like a blueberry," said Mr. Wonka.

"Call me a doctor!" shouted Mr. Beauregarde.

"Prick her with a pin!" said one of the fathers.

"Save her!" cried Mrs. Beauregarde, wringing her hands.

But there was no saving her now. Her body was swelling up and changing shape at such a rate that within a minute it had turned into nothing less than an enormous round blue ball—a gigantic blueberry, in fact—and all that remained of Violet Beauregarde herself was a tiny pair of legs and a tiny pair of arms sticking out of the great round fruit and a little head on top.

"It always happens like that," sighed Mr. Wonka. "I've tried it twenty times in the Testing Room on twenty Oompa-Loompas, and every one of them finished up as a blueberry. It's most annoying. I just can't understand it."

"But I don't want a blueberry for a daughter!" yelled Mrs. Beauregarde. "Put her back to what she was this instant!"

Mr. Wonka clicked his fingers, and ten Oompa-Loompas appeared immediately at his side.

"Roll Miss Beauregarde into the boat," he said to them, "and take her along to the Juicing Room at once."

"The Juicing Room?" cried Mrs. Beauregarde. "What are they going to do to her there?"

"Squeeze her," said Mr. Wonka. "We've got to squeeze the juice out of her immediately. After that, we'll just have to see how she comes out. But don't worry, my dear Mrs. Beauregarde. We'll get her repaired if it's the last thing we do. I am sorry about it all, I really am . . ."

Already the ten Oompa-Loompas were rolling the enormous blueberry across the floor of the Inventing Room toward the door that led to the chocolate river where the boat was waiting. Mr. and Mrs. Beauregarde hurried after them. The rest of the party, including little Charlie Bucket and Grandpa Joe, stood absolutely still and watched them go.

"Listen!" whispered Charlie. "Listen, Grandpa! The Oompa-Loompas in the boat outside are starting to sing!"

The voices, one hundred of them singing together, came loud and clear into the room:

"Dear friends we surely all agree
There's almost nothing worse to see
Than some repulsive little bum
Who's always chewing chewing gum.
(It's very near as bad as those
Who sit around and pick the nose)
So please believe us when we say
That chewing gum will never pay;
This sticky habit's bound to send
The chewer to a sticky end.
Did any of you ever know
A person called Miss Bigelow?
This dreadful woman saw no wrong
In chewing, chewing all day long.
She chewed while bathing in the tub,
She chewed while dancing at her club,
She chewed in church and on the bus;
It really was quite ludicrous!
And when she couldn't find her gum
She'd chew up the linoleum,
Or anything that happened near—
A pair of boots, the postman's ear,
Or other people's underclothes,
And once she chewed her boyfriend's nose.
She went on chewing till, at last,
Her chewing muscles grew so vast
That from her face her giant chin
Stuck out just like a violin.
For years and years she chewed away,
Consuming fifty packs a day,
Until one summer's eve, alas,
A horrid business came to pass.
Miss Bigelow went late to bed,

For half an hour she lay and read,
Chewing and chewing all the while
Like some great clockwork crocodile.
At last, she put her gum away
Upon a special little tray,
And settled back and went to sleep—
(She managed this by counting sheep)
But now, how strange! Although she slept,
Those massive jaws of hers still kept
On chewing, chewing through the night,
Even with nothing there to bite.
They were, you see, in such a groove
They positively had to move.
And very grim it was to hear
In pitchy darkness, loud and clear,
This sleeping woman's great big trap
Opening and shutting, snap-snap-snap!
Faster and faster, chop-chop-chop,
The noise went on, it wouldn't stop.
Until at last her jaws decide
To pause and open extra wide,
And with the most tremendous chew
They bit the lady's tongue in two.
Thereafter, just from chewing gum,
Miss Bigelow was always dumb,
And spent her life shut up in some
Disgusting sanatorium.
And that is why we'll try so hard
To save Miss Violet Beauregarde
From suffering an equal fate.
She's still quite young, It's not too late,
Provided she survives the cure.
We hope she does. We can't be sure."

Tom works very hard as a chimney-sweep until one day some fairies turn him into a water-baby. He enjoys his life in the water-world but drives all the water-creatures to distraction until they get quite angry with him.

The Water-Babies: A Fairy Tale for a Land-Baby

CHARLES KINGSLEY

CHAPTER 3

Tom was now quite amphibious. You do not know what that means? You had better, then, ask the nearest teacher, who may possibly answer you smartly enough, thus "Amphibious. Adjective, derived from two Greek words, amphi, a fish, and bios, a beast. An animal supposed by our ignorant ancestors to be compounded of a fish and a beast; which, like the hippopotamus, can't live on the land, and dies in the water."

However that may be, Tom was amphibious and he was clean. For the first time in his life, he felt how comfortable it was to have nothing on him but himself. But he only enjoyed it: he did not know it, or think about it; just as you enjoy life and health, and yet never think about being alive and healthy; and may it be long before you have to think about it!

He did not remember ever having been dirty. Since that sweet sleep, he had forgotten all about his master, and Harthover Place, and the little white girl, and all that had happened to him when he lived before; and what was best of all, he had forgotten all the bad words which he had learned from Grimes and the rude boys with whom he used to play. That is not strange: for you know, when you came into this world, and became a land-baby, you remembered nothing. So why should he when he became a water-baby?

Then have you lived before? My dear child, who can tell? One can only tell that by remembering something which happened where we lived before; and as we remember nothing, we know nothing about it; and no book, and no man, can ever tell us certainly.

There was a wise man once, a very wise man, and a very good man, who wrote a poem about the feelings which some children have about having lived before; and this is what he said:

> *"Our birth is but a sleep and a forgetting;*
> *The soul that rises with us, our life's star,*
> *Hath elsewhere had its setting,*
> *And cometh from afar:*
> *Not in entire forgetfulness,*
> *And not in utter nakedness,*
> *But trailing clouds of glory do we come*
> *From God, who is our home."*

There, you can know no more than that. But if I were you, I would believe that. For then the great fairy Science, who is likely to be queen of all fairies for many a year to come, can only do you good, and never do you harm; and instead of fancying that your body makes your soul, as if a steam-engine could make its own coke; or, with some people, that your soul has nothing to do with your body, but is only stuck into it like a pin into a pincushion, to fall out with the first shake; you will believe the one true, orthodox, inductive, rational, deductive, philosophical, seductive, logical, productive, irrefragable, salutary, nonimalistic, realistic, and on-all-accounts-to-be-received doctrine of this wonderful fairy tale; which is, that your soul makes your body, just as a snail makes his shell for the rest, it is enough for us to be sure that whether or not we lived before, we shall live again; though not, I hope, as poor little heathen Tom did. For he went downward into the water: but we, I hope, shall go upward to a very different place.

But Tom was very happy in the water. He had been sadly overworked in the land-world; and so now, to make up for that, he had nothing but holidays in the water-world for a long time to come. He had nothing to do now but enjoy himself, and look at all the pretty things which are to be seen in the cool clear water-world, where the sun is never too hot, and the frost is never too cold.

And what did he live on? Water-cresses, perhaps; or perhaps water-gruel, and water-milk; too many land-babies do so likewise; sometimes he went along the smooth gravel water-ways, looking at the crickets which ran in and out among the stones, as rabbits do on land; or he climbed over the ledges of rock, and saw the sandpipes hanging in thousands, with every one of them a pretty little head and legs peeping out; or he went into a still corner, and watched the caddises eating deadsticks as greedily as you would eat plum-pudding, and building their houses with silk and glue. Very fanciful ladies they were; none of them would keep to the same materials for a day. One would begin with some pebbles; then she would stick on a piece of green wood; then she found a shell, and stuck it on too; and the poor shell was alive, and did not like at all being taken to build houses with: but the caddis did not let him have any voice in the matter, being rude and selfish, as vain people are apt to be; then she stuck on a piece of rotten wood, then a very smart pink stone, and so on, till she was patched all over like an Irishman's coat. Then she found a long straw, five times as long as herself, and said, "Hurrah, my sister has a tail, and I'll have one, too;" and she stuck it on her back, and marched about with it quite proud, though it was very inconvenient indeed.

Then sometimes he came to a deep still reach; and there he saw the water-forests; they would have looked to you only little weeds; but Tom, you must remember, was so little that everything looked a hundred times as big to him as it does to you, just as things do to a minnow, who sees and catches the little water-creatures which you can only see in a microscope.

And in the water-forest he saw the water-monkeys and water-squirrels (they had all six legs, though; everything almost has six legs in the water, except efts and water-babies); and nimbly enough they ran among the branches. There were water-flowers there, too, in thousands; and Tom tried to pick them: but as soon as he touched them, they drew themselves in and turned into knots of jelly; and then Tom saw that they were all alive—bells, and stars, and wheels, and flowers, of all beautiful shapes and colors; and all alive and busy, just as Tom was. He found that there was a deal more in the world than he had fancied at first sight.

There was one wonderful little fellow, too, who peeped out of the top of a house built of round bricks. He had two big wheels, and one little one, all over teeth, spinning round and round like the wheels in a threshing machine; and Tom stood and stared at him, to see what he was going to make with his machinery. And what do you think he was doing? Brick-making. With his two big wheels he swept together all the mud which floated in the water: all that was nice in it he put into his stomach and ate; and all the mud he put into the little wheel on his breast, which really was a round hole set with teeth; and there he spun it into a neat hard round brick; and then he took it and stuck it on the top of his house-wall, and set to work to make another. Now was not he a clever little fellow?

Tom thought so: but when he wanted to talk to him the brick-maker was much too busy to notice him.

Now you must know that all the things under the water talk; only not such a language as ours; but such as horses, and dogs, and cows, and birds talk to each other; and Tom soon learned to understand them and talk to them; so that he might have had very pleasant company if he had only been a good boy. But I am sorry to say, he was too like some other little boys, very fond of tormenting creatures for mere sport. Some people say that boys cannot help it; that it is nature, and only a proof that we are all originally descended from beasts of prey. But whether it is nature or not, little boys can help it, and must help it. For if they have naughty, mischievous tricks in their nature, as monkeys have, that is no reason why they should give way to those tricks like monkeys, who know no better. And therefore they must not torment dumb creatures; for if they do, a certain old lady who is coming will surely give them exactly what they deserve.

But Tom did not know that; and he pecked and howked the poor water-things about sadly, till they were all afraid of him, and got out of his way, or crept into their shell; so he had no one to speak to or play with. The water-fairies were sorry to see him so unhappy, and longed to take him, and tell him how naughty he was, and teach him to be good, and to play and romp with him too: but they had been forbidden to do that. Tom had to learn his lesson for himself by sound and sharp experience, as many another foolish person has to do, though there may be many a kind heart yearning over them all the while, and longing to teach them what they can only teach themselves.

At last one day he found a caddis, And wanted it to peep out of its house: but its house-door was shut. He had never seen a caddis with a house-door before: so what must he do, the meddlesome little fellow, but pull it open, to see what the poor lady was doing inside. What a shame!

How should you like to have any one breaking your bedroom door in, to see how you looked when you were in bed? So Tom broke to pieces the door, which was the prettiest little grating of silk, stuck all over with shining bits of crystal; and when he looked in, the caddis poked out her head, and it had turned into just the shape of a bird's. But when Tom spoke to her she could not answer; for her mouth and face were tight tied up in a new night-cap of neat pink skin. However, if she didn't answer, all the other caddises did; for they held up their hands and shrieked like the cats in Sturwelpeter: "Oh, you nasty, horrid boy; there you are at it again! And she had just laid herself up for a fortnight's sleep, and then she would have come out with such beautiful wings, and flown about, and laid such lots of eggs: and now you have broken her door, and she can't mend it because her mouth is tied up for a fortnight, and she will die. Who sent you here to worry us out of our lives?"

So Tom swam away. He was very much ashamed of himself, and felt all the naughtier; as little boys do when they have done wrong and won't say so.

Dr. John Dolittle lives in Puddleby-on-the Marsh. His house is filled with animals in every nook and cranny. He likes animals more than people! An old woman with rheumatism once came to see the doctor, sat on a hedgehog sleeping on the sofa, and never came to see him again. Soon he lost almost all of his people patients. Then one day, the cat's-meat man gave him some very valuable advice—why not take care of animals?

The Story of Doctor Dolittle

HUGH LOFTING

ANIMAL LANGUAGE

It happened one day that the Doctor was sitting in his kitchen talking with the cat's-meat man, who had come to see him with a stomach ache.

"Why don't you give up being a people's doctor, and be an animal doctor?" asked the cat's-meat man.

The parrot, Polynesia, was sitting in the window looking out at the rain and singing a sailor song to herself. She stopped singing and started to listen.

"You see, Doctor," the cat's-meat man went on, "you know all about animals—much more than what these here vets do. That book you wrote about cats—why, it's wonderful! I can't read or write myself, or maybe I'd write some books. But my wife, Theodosia, she's a scholar, she is. And she read your book to me. Well, it's wonderful—that's all can be said—wonderful. You might have been a cat yourself. You know the way they think. And listen: You can make a lot of money doctoring animals. Do you know what? You see, I'd send all

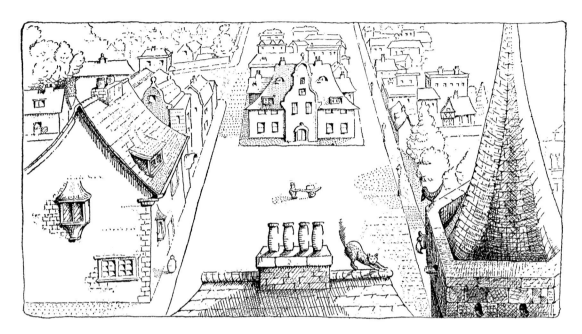

the old women who had sick cats or dogs to you. And if they didn't get sick fast enough, I could put something in the meat I sell 'em to make 'em sick, see?"

"Oh no," said the Doctor quickly. "You mustn't do that. That wouldn't be right."

"Oh, I didn't mean real sick," answered the cat's-meat man. "Just a little something to make them droopylike was what I had reference to. But as you say, maybe it ain't quite fair on the animals. But they'll get sick anyway because the old women always give 'em too much to eat. And look, all the farmers round about who had lame horses and weak lambs—they'd come. Be an animal doctor."

When the cat's-meat man had gone the parrot flew off the window onto the Doctor's table and said, "That man's got sense. That's what you ought to do. Be an animal doctor. Give the silly people up if they haven't brains enough to see you're the best doctor in the world. Take care of animals instead. They'll soon find it out. Be an animal doctor."

"Oh, there are plenty of animal doctors," said John Dolittle, putting the flower pots outside on the windowsill to get the rain.

"Yes, there are plenty," said Polynesia. "But none of them are any good at all. Now listen, Doctor, and I'll tell you something. Did you know that animals can talk?"

"I know that parrots can talk," said the Doctor.

"Oh, we parrots can talk in two languages—people's language and bird language," said

Polynesia proudly. "If I say 'Polly wants a cracker,' you understand me. But hear this: Ka-ka oi-ee, fee-fee?"

"Good gracious!" cried the Doctor. "What does that mean?"

"That means 'is the porridge hot yet?' in bird language."

"My! You don't say so!" said the Doctor. "You never talked that way to me before."

"What would have been the good?" said Polynesia, dusting some cracker crumbs off her left wing. "You wouldn't have understood me if I had."

"Tell me some more," said the Doctor, all excited, and he rushed over to the dresser drawer and came back with the butcher's book and a pencil. "Now, don't go too fast and I'll write it down. This is interesting, very interesting—something quite new. Give me the Birds' ABC first—slowly, now."

So that was the way the Doctor came to know that animals had a language of their own and could talk to one another. And all that afternoon, while it was raining, Polynesia sat on the kitchen table giving him bird words to put down in the book.

At teatime, when the dog, Jip, came in, the parrot said to the Doctor, "See, he's talking to you."

"Looks to me as though he were scratching his ear," said the Doctor.

"But animals don't always speak with their mouths," said the parrot in a high voice, raising her eyebrows. "They talk with their ears, with their feet, with their tails—with everything. Sometimes they don't want to make a noise. Do you see now the way he's twitching up one side of his nose?"

"What's that mean?" asked the Doctor.

"That means 'Can't you see that it has stopped raining?'" Polynesia answered. "He is asking you a question. Dogs nearly always use their noses for asking questions."

After a while, with the parrot's help, the Doctor got to learn the language of the animals so well that he could talk to them himself and understand everything they said. Then he gave up being a people's doctor altogether.

As soon as the cat's-meat man had told everyone that John Dolittle was going to become an animal doctor, old ladies began to bring him their pet pugs and poodles who had eaten too much cake, and farmers came many miles to show him sick cows and sheep.

One day a plow horse was brought to him, and the poor thing was terribly glad to find a man who could talk in horse language.

"You know, Doctor," said the horse, "that vet over the hill knows nothing at all. He

has been treating me six weeks now—for spavins. What I need is spectacles. I am going blind in one eye. There's no reason why horses shouldn't wear glasses the same as people. But that stupid man over the hill never even looked at my eyes. He kept on giving me big pills. I tried to tell him, but he couldn't understand a word of horse language. What I need is spectacles."

"Of course, of course," said the Doctor. "I'll get you some at once."

"I would like a pair like yours," said the horse, "only green. They'll keep the sun out of my eyes while I'm plowing the 50-acre field."

"Certainly," said the Doctor. "Green ones you shall have."

"You know, the trouble is, sir," said the plow horse as the Doctor opened the front door to let him out, "the trouble is that anybody thinks he can doctor animals, just because the animals don't complain. As a matter of fact, it takes a much cleverer man to be a really good animal doctor than it does to be a good people's doctor. My farmer's boy thinks he knows all about horses. I wish you could see him. His face is so fat he looks as though he had no eyes, and he has got as much brain as a potato bug. He tried to put a mustard plaster on me last week."

"Where did he put it?" asked the Doctor.

"Oh, he didn't put it anywhere—on me," said the horse. "He only tried to. I kicked him into the duck pond."

"Well, well!" said the Doctor.

"I'm a pretty quiet creature as a rule," said the horse, "very patient with people, don't make much fuss. But it was bad enough to have that vet giving me the wrong medicine. And when that red-faced booby started to monkey with me, I just couldn't bear it anymore."

"Did you hurt the boy much?" asked the Doctor.

"Oh, no," said the horse. "I kicked him in the right place. The vet's looking after him now. When will my glasses be ready?"

"I'll have them for you next week," said the Doctor. "Come in again Tuesday. Good morning!"

Then John Dolittle got a fine big pair of green spectacles, and the plow horse stopped going blind in one eye and could see as well as ever.

And soon it became a common sight to see farm animals wearing glasses in the country around Puddleby, and a blind horse was a thing unknown.

And so it was with all the other animals that were brought to him. As soon as they found that he could talk their language, they told him where the pain was and how they felt, and of course it was easy for him to cure them.

Now all these animals went back and told their brothers and friends that there was a doctor in the little house with the big garden who really was a doctor. And whenever any creatures got sick—not only horses and cows and dogs, but all the little things of the fields, like harvest mice and water voles, badgers and bats—they came at once to his house on the edge of the town, so that his big garden was nearly always crowded with animals trying to get in to see him.

There were so many that came that he had to have special doors made for the different

kinds. He wrote HORSES over the front door, COWS over the side door, and SHEEP on the kitchen door. Each kind of animal had a separate door—even the mice had a tiny tunnel made for them into the cellar, where they waited patiently in rows for the Doctor to come around to them.

And so, in a few years' time, every living thing for miles and miles got to know about John Dolittle, M.D. And the birds who flew to other countries in the winter told the animals in foreign lands of the wonderful doctor of Puddleby-on-the-Marsh, who could understand their talk and help them in their troubles. In this way he became famous among the animals all over the world, better known even than he had been among the folks of the West Country. And he was happy and liked his life very much.

One afternoon when the Doctor was busy writing in a book, Polynesia sat in the window, as she nearly always did, looking out at the leaves blowing about in the garden. Presently she laughed aloud.

"What is it, Polynesia?" asked the Doctor, looking up from his book.

"I was just thinking," said the parrot, and she went on looking at the leaves.

"What were you thinking?"

"I was thinking about people," said Polynesia. "People make me sick. They think they're so wonderful. The world has been going on now for thousands of years, hasn't it? And the only thing in animal language that people have learned to understand is that when a dog wags his tail he means 'I'm glad!' It's funny, isn't it? You are the very first man to talk like us. Oh, sometimes people annoy me dreadfully—such airs they put on talking about 'the dumb animals.' Dumb! Huh! Why, I knew a macaw once who could say good morning in seven different ways without once opening his mouth. He could talk every language—and Greek. An old professor with a gray beard bought him. But he didn't stay. He said the old man didn't talk Greek right, and he couldn't stand listening to him teach the language wrong. I often wonder what's become of him. That bird knew more geography than people will ever know. People! Golly! I suppose if people ever learn to fly—like any common hedge sparrow—we shall never hear the end of it!"

"You're a wise old bird," said the Doctor. "How old are you really? I know that parrots and elephants sometimes live to be very, very old."

"I can never be quite sure of my age," said Polynesia. "It's either 183 or 182. But I know that when I first came here from Africa, King Charles was still hiding in the oak tree—because I saw him. He looked scared to death."

Buck is a sled dog who has been kidnapped from his home in California, taken to the Canadian Arctic, and sold to men who are searching for wealth in the days of the gold rush. He learns to survive in the wild and becomes the leader of a team of dogs. Jack London gives us a harsh and brutal look into the existence of animals and humans at their most primitive level—fighting for their lives and existence.

The Call of the Wild

JACK LONDON

CHAPTER 2
THE LAW OF CLUB AND FANG

Buck's first day on the Dyea beach was like a nightmare. Every hour was filled with shock and surprise. He had been suddenly jerked from the heart of civilization and flung into the heart of things primordial. No lazy, sunkissed life was this, with nothing to do but loaf and get bored. Here was neither peace, nor rest, nor a moment's safety. All was confusion and action, and every moment life and limb were in peril. There was imperative need to be constantly alert; for these dogs and men were not town dogs and men. They were savages, all of them, who knew no law but the law of club and fang.

It was the wolf manner of fighting, to strike and leap away; but there was more to it than this. Thirty or forty huskies ran to the spot and surrounded the combatants in an intent and silent circle. Buck did not comprehend that silent intentness, nor the eager way with which they were licking their chops. Curly rushed her antagonist,

who struck again and leaped aside. He met her next rush with his chest, in a peculiar fashion that tumbled her off her feet. She never regained them. This was what the onlooking huskies had waited for. They closed in upon her, snarling and yelping, and she was buried, screaming with agony, beneath the bristling mass of bodies.

So sudden was it, and so unexpected, that Buck was taken aback. He saw Spitz run out his scarlet tongue in a way he had of laughing; and he saw Francois, swinging an axe, spring into the mess of dogs. Three men with clubs were helping him to scatter them. It did not take long. Two minutes from the time Curly went down, the last of her assailants were clubbed off. But she lay there limp and lifeless in the bloody, trampled snow, almost literally torn to pieces, the swart half-breed standing over her and cursing horribly. The scene often came back to Buck to trouble him in his sleep. So that was the way. No fair play. Once down, that was the end of you. Well, he would see to it that he never went down. Spitz ran out his tongue and laughed again, and from that moment Buck hated him with a bitter and deathless hatred.

Before he had recovered from the shock caused by the tragic passing of Curly, he received another shock. Francois fastened upon him an arrangement of straps and buckles. It was a harness, such as he had seen the grooms put on the horses at home. And as he had seen horses work, so he was set to work, hauling Francois on a sled to the forest that fringed the valley, and returning with a load of firewood. Buck learned easily, and under the combined tuition of his two mates and Francois made remarkable progress. Ere they returned to camp he knew enough to stop at "ho," to go ahead at "mush," to swing wide on the bends, and to keep clear of the wheeler when the loaded sled shot downhill at their heels.

"T'ree vair' good dogs," Francois told Perrault. "Dat Buck, heem pool lak hell. I tich heem queek as anyt'ing."

 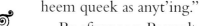

By afternoon, Perrault, who was in a hurry to be on the trail with his dispatches, returned with two more dogs. "Billee" and "Joe" he called them, two brothers, and true huskies both. Sons of the one mother though they were, they were as different as day and night. Billee's one fault was his excessive good nature, while Joe was the very opposite, sour and introspective, with a perpetual snarl and a malignant eye. Buck received them in comradely fashion, Dave ignored them, while Spitz proceeded to thrash first one and then the other.

Billee wagged his tail appeasingly, turned to run when he saw that appeasement was of no avail, and cried (still appeasingly) when Spitz's sharp teeth scored his flank. But no matter how Spitz circled, Joe whirled around on his heels to face him, mane bristling, ears laid back, lips writhing and snarling, jaws clipping together as fast as he could snap, and eyes diabolically gleaming—the incarnation of belligerent fear. So terrible was his appearance that Spitz was forced to forego disciplining him; but to cover his own discomfiture he turned upon the inoffensive and wailing Billee and drove him to the confines of the camp.

"JOE"

By evening Perrault secured another dog, an old husky, long and lean and gaunt, with a battle-scarred face and a single eye which flashed a warning of prowess that commanded respect. He was called Sol-leks, which means the Angry One. Like Dave, he asked nothing, gave nothing, expected nothing; and when he marched slowly and deliberately into their midst, even Spitz left him alone. He had one peculiarity which Buck was unlucky enough to discover. He did not like to be approached on his blind side. Of this offense Buck was unwittingly guilty, and the first knowledge he had of his indiscretion was when Sol-leks whirled upon him and slashed his shoulder to the bone for three inches up and down. Forever after Buck avoided his blind side, and to the last of their comradeship had no more trouble. His only apparent ambition, like Dave's, was to be left alone; though, as Buck was afterward to learn, each of them possessed one other and even more vital ambition.

That night Buck faced the great problem of sleeping. The tent, illumined by a candle, glowed warmly in the midst of the white plain; and when he, as a matter of course, entered it, both Perrault and Francois bombarded him with curses and cooking utensils, till he recovered from his consternation and fled ignominiously into the outer cold. A chill wind was blowing that nipped him sharply and bit with especial venom into his wounded shoulder. He lay down on the snow and attempted to sleep, but the frost soon drove him shivering to his feet. Miserable and disconsolate, he wandered about among the many tents, only to find that one place was as cold as another. Here and there savage dogs rushed upon him, but he bristled his neck-hair and snarled (for he was learning fast), and they let him go his way unmolested.

Finally an idea came to him. He would return and see how his own teammates were making out. To his astonishment, they had disappeared. Again he wandered about through the great camp, looking for them, and again he returned. Were they in the tent? No, that could not be, else he would not have been driven out. Then where could they possibly be? With drooping tail and shivering body, very forlorn indeed, he aimlessly circled the tent. Suddenly the snow gave way beneath his fore legs and he sank down. Something wriggled under his feet. He sprang back, bristling and snarling, fearful of the unseen and unknown. But a friendly little yelp reassured him, and he went back to investigate. A whiff of warm air ascended to his nostrils, and there, curled up under the snow in a snug ball, lay Billee. He whined placatingly, squirmed and wriggled to show his good will and intentions, and even ventured, as a bribe for peace, to lick Buck's face with his warm wet tongue.

Another lesson. So that was the way they did it, eh? Buck confidently selected a spot, and with much fuss and wasted effort proceeded to dig a hole for himself. In a trice the heat from his body filled the confined space and he was asleep. The day had been long and arduous, and he slept soundly and comfortably, though he growled and barked and wrestled with bad dreams.

Nor did he open his eyes till roused by the noises of the waking camp. At first he did not know where he was. It had snowed during the night and he was completely buried. The snow walls pressed him on every side, and a great surge of fear swept through him— the fear of the wild thing for the trap. It was a token that he was harking back through his own life to the lives of his forebears; for he was a civilized dog, an unduly civilized dog, and of his own experience knew no trap and so could not of himself fear it. The muscles of his whole body contracted spasmodically and instinctively, the hair on his neck and shoulders stood on end, and with a ferocious snarl he bounded straight up into the blinding day, the snow flying about him in a flashing cloud. Ere he landed on his feet, he saw the white camp spread out before him and knew where he was and remembered all that had passed from the time he went for a stroll with Manuel to the hole he had dug for himself the night before.

A shout from Francois hailed his appearance. "Wot I say?" the dog-driver cried to Perrault. "Dat Buck for sure learn queek as anyt'ing."

Perrault nodded gravely. As courier for the Canadian government, bearing important dispatches, he was anxious to secure the best dogs, and he was particularly gladdened by the possession of Buck.

In the nineteenth century Anna Sewell explored a horse's thoughts and emotions by having Black Beauty narrate his own tale. The following two excerpted chapters from the novel *Black Beauty* provide a view into Black Beauty's impressions of life as a young colt, and then as an older horse, seasoned through the years.

Black Beauty

ANNA SEWELL

CHAPTER 1
MY EARLY HOME

The first place that I can well remember was a large pleasant meadow with a pond of clear water in it. Some shady trees leaned over it, and rushes and water-lilies grew at the deep end. Over the hedge on one side we looked into a ploughed field, and on the other we looked over a gate at our master's house, which stood by the roadside; at the top of the meadow was a grove of fir trees, and at the bottom a running brook overhung by a steep bank.

Whilst I was young, I lived upon my mother's milk, as I could not eat grass. In the daytime I ran by her side, and at night I lay down close by her. When it was hot, we used to stand by the pond in the shade of the trees, and when it was cold, we had a nice warm shed near the grove.

As soon as I was old enough to eat grass, my mother used to go out to work in the daytime, and come back in the evening.

There were six young colts in the meadow besides me; they were older than I was: some were nearly as large as grown-up horses. I used to run

MY EARLY HOME

with them, and had great fun; we used to gallop all together round and round the field as hard as we could go. Sometimes we had rather rough play, for they would frequently bite and kick as well as gallop.

One day, when there was a good deal of kicking, my mother whinnied to me to come to her, and then she said, "I wish you to pay attention to what I am going to say to you. The colts who live here are very good colts, but they are cart-horse colts, and of course they have not learned manners. You have been well-bred and well-born; your father has a great name in these parts, and your grandfather won the cup two years at the New-market races; your grandmother had the sweetest temper of any horse I ever knew, and I think you have never seen me kick or bite. I hope you will grow up gentle and good, and never learn bad ways; do your work with a good will, lift your feet up well when you trot, and never bite or kick, even in play."

I have never forgotten my mother's advice; I knew she was a wise old horse, and our master thought a great deal of her. Her name was Duchess, but he often called her Pet.

Our master was a good, kind man. He gave us good food, good lodging, and kind words; he spoke as kindly to us as he did to his little children. We were all fond of him, and my mother loved him very much. When she saw him at the gate, she would neigh with joy, and trot up to him. He would pat and stroke her and say, "Well, old Pet, and how is your little Darkie?" I was a dull black, so he called me Darkie; then he would give me a piece of bread, which was very good, and sometimes he brought me a carrot for my mother. All the horses would come to him, but I think we were his favorites. My mother always took him to town on a market day in a light gig.

There was a ploughboy, Dick, who sometimes came into our field to pluck blackberries from the hedge. When he had eaten all he wanted, he would have what he called fun with the colts, throwing stones and sticks at them to make them gallop. We did not much mind him, for we could gallop off; but sometimes a stone would hit and hurt us.

One day he was at this game, and did not know that the master was in the next field; but he was there, watching what was going on; over the hedge he jumped in a snap, and catching Dick by the arm, he gave such a box on the ear as made him roar with the pain and surprise. As soon as we saw the master, we trotted up nearer to see what went on.

"Bad boy!" he said, "Bad boy! To chase the colts. This is not the first time, nor the second, but it shall be the last. There—take your money and go home; I shall not want you on my farm again." So we never saw Dick any more. Old Daniel, the man who looked after the horses, was just as gentle as our master, so we were well off.

CHAPTER 5
A FAIR START

The name of the coachman was John Manley; he had a wife and one little child, and they lived in the coachman's cottage, very near the stables.

The next morning he took me into the yard and gave me a good grooming, and just as I was going into my box, with my coat soft and bright, the Squire came in to look at me, and seemed pleased. "John," he said, "I meant to have tried the new horse this morning, but I have other business. You may as well take him around after breakfast; go by the common and the Highwood, and back by the watermill and the river; that will show his paces."

"I will, sir," said John. After breakfast he came and fitted me with a bridle. He was very particular in letting out and taking in the straps, to fit my head comfortably; then he brought a saddle, but it was not broad enough for my back; he saw it in a minute and went for another, which fitted nicely. He rode me first slowly, then a trot, then a canter, and when we were on the common he gave me a light touch with his whip, and we had a splendid gallop.

"Ho, ho! my boy," he said, as he pulled me up, "you would like to follow the hounds, I think."

As we came back through the park we met the Squire and Mrs. Gordon walking; they stopped, and John jumped off.

"Well, John, how does he go?"

"First-rate, sir," answered John; "he is as fleet as a deer, and has a fine spirit too; but the lightest touch of the rein will guide him. Down at the end of the common we met one of those traveling carts hung all over with baskets, rugs, and such like; you know, sir, many horses will not pass those carts quietly; he just took a good look at it, and then went on as quiet and pleasant as could be. The were shooting rabbits near the Highwood, and a gun went off close by; he pulled up a little and looked, but did not stir a step to right or left. I just held the rein steady but did not hurry him, and it's my opinion he has not been frightened or ill-used while he was young."

"That's well," said the Squire, "I will try him myself tomorrow."

The next day I was brought up for my master. I remembered my mother's counsel and my good old master's, and I tried to do exactly what he wanted me to do. I found he was a very good rider, and thoughtful for his horse too. When he came home, the lady was at the hall door as he rode up.

"Well, my dear," she said, "how do you like him?"

"He is exactly what John said," he replied; "a pleasanter creature I never wish to mount. What shall we call him?"

"Would you like Ebony?" said she; "he is as black as ebony."

"No, not Ebony."

"Will you call him Blackbird, like your uncle's old horse?"

"No, he is far handsomer than old Blackbird ever was."

"Yes," she said, "he is really quite a beauty, and he has such a sweet, good-tempered face and such a fine intelligent eye—what do you say to calling him Black Beauty?"

"Black Beauty—why, yes, I think that is a very good name. If you like it, it shall be his name"; and so it was.

When John went into the stable, he told James that master and mistress had chosen a good, sensible English name for me, that meant something; not like Marengo, or Pegasus, or Abdullah. They both laughed, and James said, "If it was not for bringing back the past, I should have named him Rob Roy, for I never saw two horses more alike."

"That's no wonder," said John; "didn't you know that farmer Grey's old Duchess was the mother of them both?"

I had never heard that before; and so poor Rob Roy who was killed at the last hunt was my brother! I did not wonder that my mother was so troubled. It seems that horses have no relations; at least they never know each other after they are sold.

John seemed very proud of me; he used to make my mane and tail almost as smooth as a lady's hair, and he would talk to me a great deal; of course I did not understand all he said, but I learned more and more to know what he meant, and what he wanted me to do. I grew very fond of him, he was so gentle and kind; he seemed to know just how a horse feels, and when he cleaned me he knew the tender places and the ticklish places; when he brushed my head, he went as carefully over my eyes as if they were his own, and never stirred up any ill-temper.

James Howard, the stable boy, was just as gentle and pleasant in his way, so I thought myself well off. There was another man who helped in the yard, but he had very little to do with Ginger and me.

A few days after this I had to go out with Ginger in the carriage. I wondered how we should get on together; but except laying her ears back when I was led up to her, she behaved very well. She did her work honestly, and did her full share, and I never wish to have a better partner in double harness. When we came to a hill, instead of slackening her pace, she would throw her weight right into the collar, and pull away straight up. We had both the same sort of courage at our work, and John had oftener to hold us in than to urge us forward; he never had to use the whip with either of us; then our paces were much the same, and I found it easy to keep step with her when trotting, which made it pleasant, and master always liked it when we kept step well, and so did John. After we had been out two or three times together we grew quite friendly and sociable, which made me feel very much at home.

As for Merrylegs, he and I soon became great friends; he was such a cheerful, plucky, good-tempered little fellow that he was a favorite with everyone, especially with Miss Jessie and Flora, who used to ride him about in the orchard, and have fine games with him and their little dog Frisky.

Our master had two other horses that stood in another stable. One was Justice, a roan cob, used for riding, or for the luggage cart; the other was an old brown hunter named Sir Oliver; he was past work now, but was a great favorite with the master, who gave him the run of the park; he sometimes did a little light carting on the estate, or carried one of the young ladies when they rode out with her father; for he was very gentle, and could be trusted with a child as well as Merrylegs. The cob was a strong, well-made, good-tempered horse, and we sometimes had a little chat in the paddock, but of course I could not be so intimate with him as with Ginger, who stood in the same stable.

In this collection of stories, Rudyard Kipling explains some of the strange and wonderful mysteries of nature, such as *How the Camel Got His Hump* and *How the Whale Got His Throat.*

In *The Elephant's Child* we learn that it's because of one curious little elephant that all elephants now have long trunks. In *The Beginning of the Armadillos* a confused jaguar ends up creating a whole new kind of animal. And, in *The Sing-Song of Old Man Kangaroo* we finally understand why the kangaroo can hop so far and so fast.

Just So Stories

RUDYARD KIPLING

THE ELEPHANT'S CHILD

In the High and Far-Off Times the Elephant, O Best Beloved, had no trunk. He had only a blackish, bulgy nose, as big as a boot, that he could wriggle about from side to side; but he couldn't pick up things with it. But there was one Elephant—a new Elephant—an Elephant's Child— who was full of 'satiable curiosity, and that means he asked ever so many questions. And he

lived in Africa, and he filled all Africa with his 'satiable curiosities. He asked his tall aunt, the Ostrich, why her tail-feathers grew just so, and his tall aunt the Ostrich spanked him with her hard, hard claw. He asked his tall uncle, the Giraffe, what made his skin spotty, and his tall uncle, the Giraffe, spanked him with his hard, hard hoof. And still he was full of 'satiable curiosity! He asked his broad aunt, the Hippopotamus, why her eyes were red, and his broad aunt, the Hippopotamus, spanked him with her broad, broad hoof; and he asked his hairy uncle, the Baboon, why melons tasted just so, and his hairy uncle, the Baboon, spanked him with his hairy, hairy paw. And still he was full of 'satiable curiosity! He asked questions about everything that he saw, or heard, or felt, or smelt, or touched, and all his uncles and his aunts spanked him. And still he was full of 'satiable curiosity!

One fine morning in the middle of the Precession of the Equinoxes this 'satiable Elephant's Child asked a new fine question that he had never asked before. He asked, "What does the Crocodile have for dinner?" Then everybody said, "Hush!" in a loud and dretful tone, and they spanked him immediately and directly, without stopping, for a long time.

By and by, when that was finished, he came upon Kolokolo Bird sitting in the middle of a wait-a-bit thorn-bush, and he said, "My father has spanked me, and my mother has spanked; all my aunts and uncles have spanked me for my 'satiable curiosity; and still I want to know what the Crocodile has for dinner!"

Then Kolokolo Bird said, with a mournful cry, "Go to the banks of the great gray-green, greasy Limpopo River, all set about with fever-trees, and find out."

That very next morning, when there was nothing left of the Equinoxes, because the Precession had preceded according to precedent, this 'satiable Elephant's Child took a hundred pounds of bananas (the little short red kind), and a hundred pounds of sugar-cane (the long purple kind), and seventeen melons (the greeny-crackly kinds), and said to all his dear families, "Good-bye. I am going to the great gray-green, greasy Limpopo River, all set about with fever-trees, to find out what the Crocodile has for dinner." And they all spanked him once more for luck, though he asked them most politely to stop.

Then he went away, a little warm, but not at all astonished, eating melons, and throwing the rind about, because he could not pick it up.

He went from Graham's Town to Kimberley, and from Kimberley to Khama's Country, and from Khama's Country he went east by north, eating melons all the time, till at last he came to the banks of the great gray-green, greasy Limpopo River, all set about with fever-trees, precisely as Kolokolo Bird had said.

Now you must know and understand, O Best Beloved, that till that very week, and day, and hour, and minute, this 'satiable Elephant's Child had never seen a Crocodile, and did not know what one was like. It was all his 'satiable curiosity.

The first thing that he found was a Bi-Colored-Python-Rock-Snake curled round a rock.

" 'Scuse me," said the Elephant's Child most politely, "but have you seen such a thing as a Crocodile in these promiscuous parts?"

"Have I seen a Crocodile?" said the Bi-Colored-Python-Rock-Snake, in a voice of dretful scorn. "What will you ask me next?"

" 'Scuse me," said the Elephant's Child, "but could you kindly tell me what he has for dinner?"

Then the Bi-Colored-Python-Rock-Snake uncoiled himself very quickly from the rock, and spanked the Elephant's Child with his scalesome, flailsome tail.

"That is odd," said the Elephant's Child, "because my father and my mother, and my uncle and my aunt, not to mention my other aunt, the Hippopotamus, and my other uncle, the Baboon, have all spanked me for my 'satiable curiosity—and I suppose this is the same thing."

So he said good-bye very politely to the Bi-Colored-Python-Rock-Snake, and helped to coil him up on the rock again, and went on, a little warm, but not at all astonished, eating melons, and throwing the rind about, because he could not pick it up, till he trod on what he thought was a log of wood at the very edge of the great gray-green Limpopo River, all set about with fever-trees.

But it was really the Crocodile, O Best Beloved, and the Crocodile winked one eye— like this!

" 'Scuse me," said the Elephant's Child most politely, "but do you happen to have seen a crocodile in these promiscuous parts?"

Then the Crocodile winked the other eye, and lifted half his tail out of the mud; and the Elephant's Child stepped back most politely, because he did not wish to be spanked again.

"Come hither, Little One," said the Crocodile. "Why do you ask such things?"

" 'Scuse me," said the Elephant's Child most politely, "but my father has spanked me, my mother has spanked me, not to mention my tall aunt, the Ostrich, and my tall uncle, the Giraffe, who can kick ever so hard, as well as my broad aunt the Hippopotamus, and

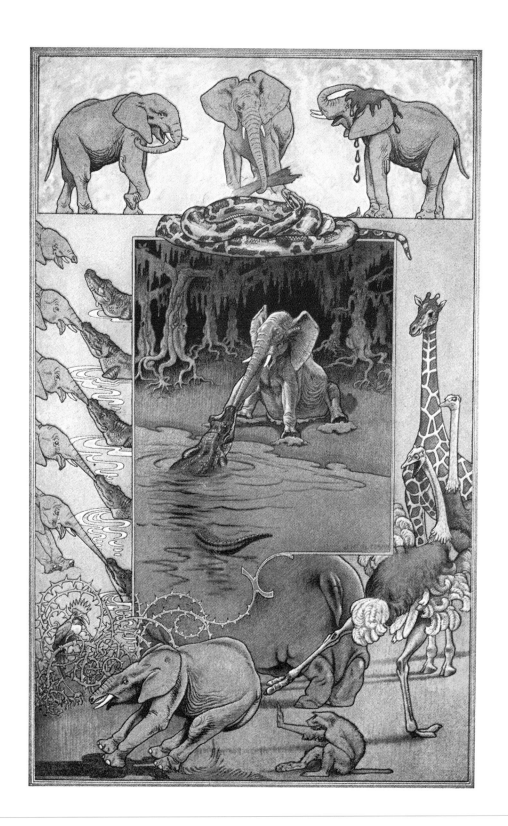

my hairy uncle, the Baboon, and including the Bi-Colored-Python-Rock-Snake, with the scalesome, flailsome tail, just up the bank, who spanks harder than any of them; and so, if it's quite all the same to you, I don't want to be spanked any more."

"Come hither, Little One," said the Crocodile, "for I am the Crocodile," and he wept crocodile-tears to show it was quite true.

Then the Elephant's Child grew all breathless, and panted, and kneeled down on the banks and said, "You are the very person I have been looking for all these long days. Will you please tell me what you have for dinner?"

"Come hither, Little One," said the Crocodile, "and I'll whisper."

Then the Elephant's Child put his head down close to the Crocodile's musky, tusky mouth, and the Crocodile caught him by his little nose, which up to that very week, day, hour, and minute, had been no bigger than a boot, though much more useful.

"I think," said the Crocodile—and he said it between his teeth, like this—"I think today I will begin with Elephant's Child!"

At this, O Best Beloved, the Elephant's Child was much annoyed, and he said speaking through his nose, like this: "Led go! You are hurtig be!"

Then the Bi-Colored-Python-Rock-Snake scuffled down from the bank and said, "My young friend, if you do not now, immediately and instantly, pull as hard as ever you can, it is my opinion that your acquaintance in the large-pattern leather ulster"—and by this he meant the Crocodile—"will jerk you into yonder limpid stream before you can say Jack Robinson."

This is the way Bi-Colored-Python-Rock-Snakes always talk.

Then the Elephant's Child sat back on his little haunches, and pulled, and pulled, and pulled, and his nose began to stretch. And the Crocodile floundered into the water, making it all creamy with great sweeps of his tail, and he pulled, and pulled, and pulled.

And the Elephant's Child's nose kept on stretching; and the Elephant's Child spread all his little four legs and pulled, and pulled, and pulled, and his nose kept on stretching; and the Crocodile threshed his tail like an oar, and he pulled, and pulled, and pulled, and at each pull the Elephant's Child's nose grew longer and longer—and it hurt him hijjus!

Then the Elephant's Child felt his legs slipping, and he said through his nose, which was now nearly five feet long, "This is too butch for be!"

Then the Bi-Colored-Python-Rock-Snake came down from the bank, and knotted himself in a double-clove hitch round the Elephant's Child's hind-legs, and said, "Rash and inexperienced traveler, we will now seriously devote ourselves to a little high tension, because if we do not, it is my impression that yonder self-propelling man-of-war with the armour-plated upper deck"—and by this, O Best Beloved, he meant the Crocodile—"will permanently vitiate your future career."

That is the way all Bi-Colored-Python-Rock-Snakes always talk.

So he pulled, and the Elephant's Child pulled, and the Crocodile pulled; but the Elephant's Child and the Bi-Colored-Python-Rock-Snake pulled hardest; and at last the Crocodile let go of the Elephant's Child's nose with a plop that you could hear all up and down the Limpopo.

Then the Elephant's Child sat down most hard and sudden; but first he was careful to say "Thank you" to the Bi-Colored-Python-Rock-Snake; and next he was kind to his poor pulled nose, and wrapped it all up in cool banana leaves, and hung it in the great gray-geen, greasy Limpopo to cool.

HOW THE CAMEL GOT HIS HUMP

Now this is the next tale, and it tells how the Camel got his big hump.

In the beginning of years, when the world was so new-and-all, and the Animals were just beginning to work for Man, there was a Camel, and he lived in the middle of a Howling Desert because he did not want to work; and besides, he was a Howler himself. So he ate sticks and thorns and tamarisks and milkweed and prickles, most 'scruciating idle; and when anybody spoke to him he said "Humph!" Just "Humph!" and no more.

Presently the Horse came to him on Monday morning, with a saddle on his back and a bit in his mouth, and said, "Camel, O Camel, come out and trot like the rest of us."

"Humph!" said the Camel; and the Horse went away and told the Man.

Presently the Dog came to him, with a stick in his mouth, and said, "Camel, O Camel, come and fetch and carry like the rest of us."

"Humph!" said the Camel; and the Horse went away and told the man.

Presently the Ox came to him, with the yoke on his neck, and said, "Camel, O Camel; come and plough like the rest of us."

"Humph!" said the Camel; and the Ox went away and told the Man.

At the end of the day the Man called the Horse and the Dog and the Ox together, and said, "Three, O Three, I'm very sorry for you (with the world so new-and-all); but that Humph-thing in the Desert can't work, or he would have been here by now, so I am going to leave him alone, and you must work double-time to make up for it."

That made the Three very angry (with the world so new-and-all), and they held a palaver, and an indaba, and a punchayet, and a pow-wow on the edge of the Desert; and the Camel came chewing milkweed most 'scruciating idle, and laughed at them. Then he said "Humph!" and went away again.

Presently there came along the Djinn in charge of All Deserts, rolling in a cloud of dust (Djinns always travel that way because it is Magic), and he stopped to palaver and pow-wow with the Tree.

"Djinn of All Deserts," said the Horse, "is it right for any one to be idle, with the world so new-and-all!?"

"Certainly not," said the Djinn.

"Well," said the Horse, "there's a thing in the middle of your Howling Desert (and he's

a Howler himself) with a long neck and long legs, and he hasn't done a stroke of work since Monday morning. He won't trot."

"Whew!" said the Djinn, whistling, "that's my Camel, for all the gold in Arabia! What does he say about it?"

"He says, 'Humph!'" said the Dog; "and he won't fetch and carry."

"Does he say anything else?"

"Only 'Humph!'; and he won't plough," said the Ox.

"Very good," said the Djinn. "I'll humph him if you will kindly wait a minute."

The Djinn rolled himself up in his dust-cloak, and took a bearing across the desert, and found the Camel most 'scruciatingly idle, looking at his own reflection in a pool of water.

"My long and bubbling friend," said the Djinn, "what's this I hear of your doing no work, with the world so new-and-all?"

"Humph!" said the Camel.

The Djinn sat down, with his chin in his hand, and began to think a Great Magic, while the Camel looked at his own reflection in the pool of water.

"You've given the Three extra work ever since Monday morning, all on account of your 'scruciating idleness," said the Djinn; and he went on thinking Magics, with his chin in his hand.

"Humph!" said the Camel.

"I shouldn't say that again if I were you," said the Djinn; "you might say it once too often. Bubbles, I want you to work."

And the Camel said "Humph!" again; but no sooner had he sat it than he saw his back, that he was so proud of, puffing up and puffing up into a great big lolloping humph.

"Do you see that?" said the Djinn. "That's your very own humph that you've brought upon your very own self by not working. To-day is Thursday, and you've done no work since Monday, when the work began. Now you are going to work."

"How can I," said the Camel, "with this humph on my back?"

"That's made a-purpose," said the Djinn, "all because you missed those three days. You will be able to work now for three days without eating, because you can live on your humph; and don't you ever say I never did anything for you. Come out of the Desert and go to the Three, and behave. Humph yourself!"

And the Camel humphed himself, humph and all, and went away to join the Three. And from that day to this the Camel always wears a humph (we call it "hump" now, not to hurt his feelings); but he has never yet caught up with the three days that he missed at the beginning of the world, and he has never yet learned how to behave.

The Camel's hump is an ugly lump
Which well you may see at the Zoo;
But uglier yet is the hump we get
From having too little to do.

Kiddies and grown-ups too-oo-oo,
If we haven't enough to do-oo-oo,
   We get the hump—
    Cameelious hump—
The hump that is black and blue!

We climb out of bed with a frouzly head
And a snarly-yarly voice.
We shiver and scowl and we grunt and we growl
At our bath and our boots and our toys;

And there ought to be a corner for me
(And I know there is one for you)
   When we get the hump—
    Cameelious hump—
The hump that is black and blue!

The cure for this ill is not to sit still,
Or frowst with a book by the fire;
But to take a large hoe and a shovel also,
And dig till you gently perspire;

And then you will find that the sun and the wind,
And the Djinn of the Garden too,
   Have lifted the hump—
    The horrible hump—
The hump that is black and blue!

I get it as well as you-oo-oo-
If I haven't enough to do-oo-oo!
   We all get the hump—
    Cameelious hump—
Kiddies and grown-ups too!

THE BEGINNING OF THE ARMADILLOES

This, Oh Best Beloved, is another story of the High and Far-Off Times. In the very middle of those times was a Stickly-Prickly Hedgehog, and he lived on the banks of the turbid Amazon, eating shelly snails and things. And he had a friend, a Slow-Solid Tortoise, who lived on the banks of the turbid Amazon, eating green lettuces and things. And so that was all right, Best Beloved. Do you see?

But also, and at the same time, in those High and Far-Off Times, there was a Painted Jaguar, and he lived on the banks of the turbid Amazon too; and he ate everything that he could catch. When he could not catch deer or monkeys he would eat frogs and beetles; and when he could not catch frogs and beetles he went to his Mother Jaguar, and she told him how to eat hedgehogs and tortoises.

She said to him ever so many times, graciously waving her tail, "My son, when you find a Hedgehog you must drop him into the water and then he will uncoil, and when you catch a Tortoise you must scoop him out of his shell with your paw." And so that was all right, Best Beloved.

One beautiful night on the banks of the turbid Amazon, Painted Jaguar found Stickly-Prickly Hedgehog and Slow-Solid Tortoise sitting under the trunk of a fallen tree. They could not run away, and so Stickly-Prickly curled himself up into a ball, because he was a Hedgehog, and Slow-Solid Tortoise drew in his head and feet into his shell as fast as they would go, because he was a tortoise; and so that was all right, Best Beloved. Do you see?

"Now attend to me," said Painted Jaguar, "because this is very important. My mother said that when I meet a Hedgehog I am to drop him into the water and then he will uncoil, and when I meet a Tortoise I am to scoop him out of his shell with my paw. Now which of you is a Hedgehog and which is a Tortoise? Because, to save my spots, I can't tell."

"Are you sure of what your Mummy told you?" said Stickly-Prickly Hedgehog. "Are you quite sure? Perhaps she said that when you uncoil a Tortoise you must shell him out of the water with a scoop, and when you paw a Hedgehog you must drop him on the shell."

"Are you sure of what your Mummy told you?" said Slow-and-Solid Tortoise. "Are you quite sure? Perhaps she said that when you water a Hedgehog you must drop him into your paw, and when you meet a Tortoise you must shell him till he uncoils."

"I don't think it was at all like that," said Painted Jaguar, but he felt a little puzzled; "but, please, say it again more distinctly."

"When you scoop water with your paw you uncoil it with a Hedgehog," said Stickly-Prickly. "Remember that, because it's important."

"But," said the Tortoise, "when you paw your meat you drop it into a Tortoise with a scoop. Why can't you understand?"

"You are making my spots ache," said Painted Jaguar; "and besides, I didn't want your advice at all. I only wanted to know which of you is Hedgehog and which is Tortoise."

"I shan't tell you," said Stickly-Prickly. "But you can scoop me out of my shell if you like."

"Aha!" said Painted Jaguar. "Now I know you're Tortoise. You thought I wouldn't! Now I will." Painted Jaguar darted out his paddy-paw just as Stickly-Prickly curled himself up, and of course Jaguar's paddy-paw was just filled with prickles. Worse than that, he knocked Stickly-Prickly away and away into the woods and the bushes, where it was too dark to find him. Then he put his paddy-paw into his mouth, and of course the prickles hurt him worse than ever. As soon as he could speak he said, "Now I know he isn't Tortoise at all. But"—and then he scratched his head with his un-prickly paw—"how do I know that this other is Tortoise?"

"But I am Tortoise," said Slow-and-Solid. "Your mother was quite right. She said that you were to scoop me out of my shell with your paw. Begin."

"You didn't say she said that a minute ago," said Painted Jaguar, sucking the prickles out of his paddy-paw. "You said she said something quite different."

"Well, suppose you say that I said that she said something quite different, I don't see that it makes any difference; because if she said what you said I said she said, it's just the same as if I said what she said she said. On the other hand, if you think she said that you were to uncoil me with a scoop, instead of pawing me into drops with a shell, I can't help that, can I?"

"But you said you wanted to be scooped out of your shell with my paw," said Painted Jaguar.

"If you'll think again you'll find that I didn't say anything of the kind. I said that your mother said that you were to scoop me out of my shell," said Slow-and-Solid.

"What will happen if I do?" said the Jaguar most sniffily and most cautious.

"I don't know, because I've never been scooped out of my shell before; but I tell you truly, if you want to see me swim away you've only got to drop me into the water."

"I don't believe it," said Painted Jaguar. "You've mixed up all the things my mother told me to do with the things that you asked me whether I was sure that she didn't say, till I don't know whether I'm on my head or my painted tail; and now you come and tell me something I can understand, and it makes me more mixy than before. My mother told me that I was to drop one of you two into the water, and as you seem so anxious to be dropped I think you don't want to be dropped. So jump into the turbid Amazon and be quick about it."

"I warn you that your Mummy won't be pleased. Don't tell her I didn't tell you," said Slow-and-Solid.

"If you say another word about what my mother said—" the Jaguar answered, but he had not finished the sentence before Slow-and-Solid quietly dived into the turbid Amazon, swam under water for a long way, and came out on the bank where Stickly-Prickly was waiting for him.

"That was a very narrow escape," said Stickly-Prickly. "I don't like Painted Jaguar. What did you tell him that you were?"

"I told him truthfully that I was a truthful Tortoise, but he wouldn't believe it, and he made me jump into the river to see if I was, and I was, and he is surprised. Now he's gone to tell his Mummy. Listen to him!"

They could hear Painted Jaguar roaring up and down among the trees and the bushes by the side of the turbid Amazon, till his Mummy came

"Son, son!" said his mother ever so many times, graciously waving her tail, "what have you been doing that you shouldn't have done?"

"I tried to scoop something that said it wanted to be scooped out of its shell with my paw, and my paw is full of per-ickles," said Painted Jaguar.

"Son, son!" said his mother ever so many times graciously waving her tail, "by the prickles in your paddy-paw I see that that must have been a hedgehog. You should have dropped him into the water."

"I did that to the other thing; and he said he was a Tortoise, and I didn't believe him, and it was quite true, and I haven't anything at all to eat, and I think we had better find lodgings somewhere else. They are too clever on the turbid Amazon for poor me!"

"Son, son!" said his mother ever so many times, graciously waving her tail, "now attend to me and remember what I say. A Hedgehog curls himself up into a ball and his prickles stick out every which way at once. By this you may know the Hedgehog."

"I don't like this old lady one little bit," said Stickly-Prickly, under the shadow of a large leaf. "I wonder what else she knows?"

"A Tortoise can't curl himself up," Mother Jaguar went on, ever so many times, graciously waving her tail. "He only draws his head and legs into his shell. By this you may know the Tortoise."

"I don't like this old lady at all—at all," said Slow-and-Solid Tortoise. "Even Painted Jaguar can't forget those directions. It's a great pity that you can't swim, Stickly-Prickly."

"Don't talk to me," said Stickly-Prickly. "Just think how much better it would be if you could curl up. This is a mess! Listen to Painted Jaguar."

Painted Jaguar was sitting on the banks of the turbid Amazon sucking prickles out of his paws and saying to himself—

Can't curl, but can swim—
Slow-Solid, that's him!
Curls up, but can't swim—
Stickly-Prickly, that's him!

He'll never forget that this month of Sundays," said Stickly-Prickly. "Hold up my chin, Slow-and-Solid. I'm going to try to learn to swim. It may be useful."

"Excellent!" said Slow-and-Solid; and he held up Stickly-Prickly's chin, while Stickly-Prickly kicked in the waters of the turbid Amazon.

"You'll make a fine swimmer yet," said Slow-and-Solid. "Now, if you can unlace my backplates a little, I'll see what I can do toward curling up. It may be useful."

Stickly-Prickly helped to unlace Tortoise's back-plates, so that by twisting and straining Slow-and-Solid actually managed to curl up a tiddy wee bit.

"Excellent!" said Stickly-Prickly; "but I shouldn't do any more just now. It's making you black in the face. Kindly lead me into the water once again and I'll practice that side-stroke which you say is so easy." And so Stickly-Prickly practiced, and Slow-and-Solid swam alongside.

"Excellent!" said Slow-and-Solid. "A little more practice will make you a regular whale. Now, if I may trouble you to unlace my back and front plates two holes more, I'll try that fascinating bend that you say is so easy. Won't Painted Jaguar be surprised!"

"Excellent!" said Stickly-Prickly, all wet from the turbid Amazon. "I declare, I should-n't know you from one of my own family. Two holes, I think you said? A little more expression, please, and don't grunt quite so much, or Painted Jaguar may hear us. When you've finished, I want to try that long dive which you say is so easy. Won't Painted Jaguar be surprised!"

And so Stickly-Prickly dived, and Slow-and-Solid dived alongside.

"Excellent!" said Slow-and-Solid. "A leetle more attention to holding your breath and you will be able to keep house at the bottom of the turbid Amazon. Now I'll try that exercise of wrapping my hind legs round my ears which you say is so peculiarly com-fortable. Won't Painted Jaguar be surprised!"

"Excellent!" said Stickly-Prickly. "But it's straining your back-plates a little. They are all overlapping now, instead of lying side by side."

"Oh, that's the result of exercise," said Slow-and-Solid. "I've noticed that your prickles seem to be melting into one another, and that you're growing to look rather more like a pine-cone, and less like chestnut-bur, than you used to."

"Am I?" said Stickly-Prickly. "That comes from my soaking in the water. Oh, won't Painted Jaguar be surprised!"

They went on with their exercises, each helping the other, till morning came; and when the sun was high they rested and dried themselves. Then they saw that they were both of them quite different from what they had been.

"Stickly-Prickly," said Tortoise after breakfast, "I am not what I was yesterday; but I think that I may yet amuse the Painted Jaguar."

"That was the very thing I was thinking just now," said Stickly-Prickly. "I think scales are a tremendous improvement on prickles—to say nothing of being able to swim. Oh, won't Painted Jaguar be surprised! Let's go and find him."

By and by they found Painted Jaguar, still nursing his paddy-paw that had been hurt the night before. He was so astonished that he fell three times backward over his own painted tail without stopping.

"Good morning!" said Stickly-Prickly. "And how is your dear gracious Mummy this morning?"

"She is quite well, thank you," said Painted Jaguar; "but you must forgive me if I do not at this precise moment recall your name."

"That's unkind of you," said Stickly-Prickly, "seeing that this time yesterday you tried to scoop me out of my shell with your paw."

"But you hadn't any shell. It was all prickles," said Painted Jaguar. "I know it was. Just look at my paw!"

"You told me to drop into the turbid Amazon to be drowned," said Slow-and-Solid. "Why are you so rude and forgetful today?"

"Don't you remember what your mother told you?" said Stickly-Prickly—

> *Can't curl, but can swim—*
> *Slow-Solid, that's him!*
> *Curls up, but can't swim—*
> *Stickly-Prickly, that's him!*

Then they both curled themselves up and rolled around and around Painted Jaguar till his eyes turned truly cart-wheels in his head.

Then he went to fetch his mother.

"Mother," he said, "there are two new animals in the woods today, and the one that you said couldn't swim, swims, and the one that you said couldn't curl up, curls; and they've gone shares in their prickles, I think, because both of them are scaly all over, instead of one being smooth and the other very prickly. And, besides that, they are rolling around and around in circles, and I don't feel comfy."

"Son, son!" said Mother Jaguar ever so many times, graciously waving her tail, "a Hedgehog is a Hedgehog, and can't be anything but a Hedgehog; and a Tortoise is a Tortoise, and can never be anything else."

"But it isn't a Hedgehog, and it isn't a Tortoise. It's a little bit of both, and I don't know its proper name."

"Nonsense!" said Mother Jaguar. "Everything has its proper name. I should call it 'Armadillo' till I found out the real one. And I should leave it alone."

So Painted Jaguar did as he was told, especially about leaving them alone; but the curious thing is that from that day to his, O Best Beloved, no one on the banks of the turbid Amazon has ever called Stickly-Prickly and Slow-Solid anything except Armadillo. There are Hedgehogs and Tortoises in other places, of course (there are some in my garden); but the real old and clever kind, with the scales lying lippety-lappety one over the other, like pine-cone scales, that lived on the banks of the turbid Amazon in the High and Far-Off Days, are always called Armadilloes, because they were so clever.

So that's all right, Best Beloved. Do you see?

I've never sailed the Amazon,
    I've never reached Brazil;
But the Don and Magdalena,
    They can go there when they will!

Yes, weekly from Southampton,
    Great steamers, white and gold,
Go rolling down to Rio

(Roll down—roll down to Rio!)
And I'd like to roll to Rio
Some day before I'm old!

I've never seen a Jaguar,
Nor yet an Armadill—
O dilloing in his armor,
And I s'pose I never will,

Unless I go to Rio
These wonders to behold—
Roll down—roll down to Rio—
Roll really down to Rio!
Oh, I'd love to roll to Rio
Some day before I'm old!

HOW THE WHALE GOT HIS THROAT

In the sea, once upon a time, O my Best Beloved, there was a whale, and he ate fishes. He ate the starfish and the garfish, and the crab and the dab, and the plaice and the dace, and the skate and his mate, and the mackereel and the pickereel, and the really truly twirly-whirly eel. All the fishes he could find in all the sea he ate with his mouth—so! Till at last there was only one small fish left in all the sea, and he was a small 'Stute Fish, and he swam a little behind the Whale's right ear, so as to be out of harm's way. Then the Whale stood up on his tail and said, "I'm hungry." And the small 'Stute Fish said in a small 'stute voice, "Noble and generous Cetacean, have you ever tasted Man?"

"No," said the Whale. "What is it like?"

"Nice," said the small 'Stute Fish. "Nice but nubbly."

"Then fetch me some," said the Whale, and he made the sea froth up with his tail.

"One at a time is enough," said the 'Stute Fish. "If you swim to latitude Fifty North, longitude Forty West (that is Magic), you will find, sitting on a raft, in the middle of the sea, with nothing to wear except a pair of blue canvas breeches, a pair of suspenders (you must not forget the suspenders, Best Beloved), and a jack-knife, one shipwrecked Mariner, who, it is only fair to tell you, is a man of infinite-resource-and-sagacity."

So the Whale swam and swam to latitude 50 North, longitude 40 West, as fast as he could swim, and on a raft, in the middle of the sea, with nothing to wear except a pair of blue canvas breeches, a pair of suspenders (you must particularly remember the suspenders, Best Beloved), and a jack-knife, he found one single, solitary shipwrecked Mariner, trailing his toes in the water. (He had his Mummy's leave to paddle, or else he would never have done it, because he was a man of infinite-resource-and-sagacity.)

Then the Whale opened his mouth back and back and back till it nearly touched his tail, and

he swallowed the shipwrecked Mariner, and the raft he was sitting on, and his blue canvas breeches, and the suspenders (which you must not forget), and the jack-knife-He swallowed them all down into his warm, dark, inside cupboards, and then he smacked his lips-so, and turned round three times on his tail.

But as soon as the Mariner, who was a man of infinite-resource-and-sagacity, found himself truly inside the Whale's warm, dark, inside cupboards, he stumped and he jumped and he thumped and he bumped, and he pranced and he danced, and he banged and he clanged, and he hit and he bit, and he leaped and he creeped, and he prowled and he howled, and he hopped and he dropped, and he cried and he sighed, and he crawled and he bawled, and he stepped and he leapt, and he danced hornpipes where he shouldn't, and the Whale felt most unhappy indeed. (Have you forgotten the suspenders?)

So he said to the 'Stute Fish, "This man is very nubbly, and besides he is making me hiccup. What shall I do?"

"Tell him to come out," said the 'Stute Fish.

So the Whale called down his throat to the shipwrecked Mariner, "Come out and behave yourself. I've got the hiccups."

"Nay, nay!" said the Mariner. "Not so, but far otherwise. Take me to my natal-shore and the white-cliffs-of-Albion, and I'll think about it." And he began to dance more than ever.

So the Whale swam and swam, with both flippers and his tail, as hard as he could for the hiccups; and at last he saw the Mariner's natal-shore and the white-cliffs-of-Albion, and he rushed half-way up the beach, and opened his mouth wide and wide and wide, and said, "Change here for Winchester, Ashuelot, Nashua, Keene, and stations on the Fitchburg Road"; and just as he said "Fitch" the Mariner walked out of his mouth. But while the Whale had been swimming, the Mariner, who was indeed a person of infinite-resource-and-sagacity, had taken his jack-knife and cut up the raft into a little square grating all running criss-cross, and he had tied it firm with his suspenders (now you know why you were not to forget the suspenders!), and he dragged that grating good and tight into the Whale's throat, and there it stuck! Then he recited the following Sloka, which, as you have not heard it, I will now proceed to relate—

> *By means of a grating*
> *I have stopped your ating.*

7 5

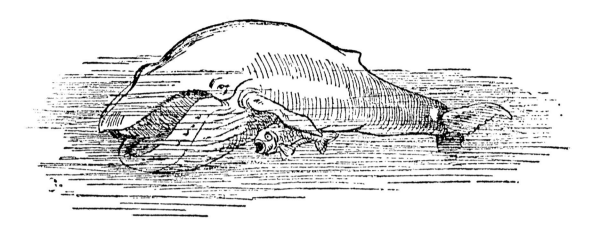

For the Mariner he was also an Hi-ber-ni-an. And he stepped out on the shingle, and went home to his Mother, who had given him leave to trail his toes in the water; and he married and lived happily ever afterward. So did the Whale. But from that day on, the grating in his throat, which he could neither cough up nor swallow down, prevented him eating anything except very, very small fish; and that is the reason why whales nowadays never eat men or boys or little girls.

The small 'Stute Fish went and hid himself in the mud under the Doorsills of the Equator. He was afraid that the Whale might be angry with him.

The Sailor took the jack-knife home. He was wearing the blue canvas breeches when he walked out on the shingle. The suspenders were left behind, you see, to tie the grating with; and that is the end of that tale.

> *When the cabin port-holes are dark and green*
> *Because of the seas outside;*
> *When the ship goes wop (with a wiggle between)*
> *And the trunks begin to slide;*
> *When the Nursey lies on the floor in a heap,*
> *And the Mummy tells you to let her sleep,*
> *And you aren't waked or washed or dressed,*
> *Why, then you will know (if you haven't guessed)*
> *You're "Fifty North and Forty West"!*

THE SING-SONG OF OLD MAN KANGAROO

Not always was the Kangaroo as now we do behold him, but a Different Animal with four short legs. He was gray and he was woolly, and his pride was inordinate: he danced on an outcrop in the middle of Australia, and he went to the Little God Nqua.

He went to Nqua at six before breakfast, saying, "Make me different from all other animals by five this afternoon."

Up jumped Nqua from his seat on the sand-flat and shouted, "Go away!"

He was gray and he was woolly, and his pride was inordinate: he danced on a rock ledge in the middle of Australia, and he went to the Middle God Nquing.

He went to Nquing at eight before breakfast, saying, "Make me different from all other animals; make me, also, wonderfully popular by five this afternoon."

Up jumped Nquing from his burrow in the spinifex and shouted, "Go away!"

He was gray and he was woolly, and his pride was inordinate: he danced on a sand-bank in the middle of Australia, and he went to the Big God Nquong.

He went to Nquong at ten before dinner-time saying, "Make me different from all other animals; make me popular and wonderfully run after by five this afternoon."

Up jumped Nquong from his bath in the salt-pan and shouted, "Yes, I will!"

Nquong called Dingo—Yellow-Dog Dingo—always hungry, dusty in the sunshine, and showed him Kangaroo. Nquong said, "Dingo! Wake up, Dingo! Do you see that gentle-man dancing on an ashpit? He wants to be popular and very truly run after. Dingo, make him so!"

Up jumped Dingo—Yellow-Dog Dingo—and said, "What, that cat-rabbit?"

Off rang Dingo—Yellow-Dog Dingo—hungry and grinning—ran after Kangaroo.

Off went the proud Kangaroo on his four little legs like a bunny.

This, O Beloved of mine, ends the first part of the tale!

He ran through the desert; he ran through the mountains; he ran through the salt-pans; he ran through the reed-beds; he ran till his front legs ached.

He had to!

Still ran Dingo—Yellow-Dog Dingo—always hungry, grinning like a rat-trap, never getting nearer, never getting farther,—ran after Kangaroo.

He had to!

Still ran Kangaroo—Old Man Kangaroo. He ran through the ti-trees; he ran through the mulga; he ran through the long grass; he ran through the short grass; he ran through the Tropics of Capricorn and Cancer; he ran till his hind legs ached.

He had to!

Still ran Dingo—Yellow-Dog Dingo—hungrier and hungrier, grinning like a horse-collar, never getting nearer, never getting farther; and they came to the Wollgong River.

Now, there wasn't any bridge, and there wasn't any ferry-boat, and Kangaroo didn't know how to get over; so he stood on his legs and hopped.

He had to!

He hopped through the Flinders; he hopped through the Cinders; he hopped through the deserts in the middle of Australia. He hopped like a Kangaroo.

First he hopped one yard; then he hopped three yards; then he hopped five yards; his legs growing stronger; his legs growing longer. He hadn't any time for rest or refreshment, and he wanted them very much.

Still ran Dingo—Yellow-Dog Dingo—very much bewildered, very much hungry, and wondering what in the world or out of it made Old Man Kangaroo hop.

For he hopped like a cricket; like a pea in a saucepan; or a new rubber ball on a nursery floor.

He had to!

He tucked up his front legs; he hopped on his hind legs; he stuck out his tail for a balance-weight behind him; and he hopped through the Darling Downs.

He had to!

Still ran Dingo—Tired-Dog Dingo—hungrier and hungrier, very much bewildered, and wondering when in the world or out of it would Old Man Kangaroo stop.

Then came Nquong from his bath in the salt-pans, and said, "It's five o'clock."

Down sat Dingo—Poor-Dog Dingo—always hungry, dusty in the sunshine; hung out his tongue and howled.

Down sat Kangaroo—Old Man Kangaroo—stuck out his tail like a milking-stool behind him, and said, "Thank goodness that's finished!"

Then said Nquong, who is always a gentleman, "Why aren't you grateful to Yellow-Dog Dingo? Why don't you thank him for all he has done for you?"

Then said the Kangaroo—Tired Old Kangaroo—"He's chased me out of the homes of my childhood; he's chased me out of my regular meal-times; he's altered my shape so

I'll never get it back; and he's played Old Scratch with my legs."

Then said Nquong, "Perhaps I'm mistaken, but didn't you ask me to make you different from all other animals, as well as to make you very truly sought after? And now it is five o'clock."

"Yes," said Kangaroo. "I wish that I hadn't. I thought you would do it by charms and incantations, but this is a practical joke."

"Joke!" said Nquong, from his bath in the blue gums. "Say that again and I'll whistle up Dingo and run your hind legs off."

"No," said the Kangaroo. "I must apologize. Legs are legs, and you needn't alter 'em so far as I am concerned. I only meant to explain to your Lordliness that I've had nothing to eat since morning, and I'm very empty indeed."

"Yes," said Dingo—Yellow-Dog Dingo—"I am just in the same situation. I've made him different from all other animals; but what may I have for my tea?"

Then said Nquong from this bath in the salt-pan, "Come and ask me about it tomorrow, because I'm going to wash."

So they were left in the middle of Australia, Old Man Kangaroo and Yellow-Dog Dingo, and each said, "That's your fault."

This is the mouth-filling song:

> *Of the race that was run by a Boomer,*
> *Run in a single burst—only event of its kind—*
> *Started by Big God Nquong from Warrigaborrigarooma,*
> *Old Man Kangaroo first: Yellow-Dog Dingo behind.*
>
> *Kangaroo bounded away,*
> *His back-legs working like pistons—*
> *Bounded from morning till dark,*
> *Twenty-five feet to a bound.*
> *Yellow-Dog Dingo lay*
> *Like a yellow cloud in the distance—*
> *Much too busy to bark.*
> *My! but they covered the ground!*

Nobody knows where they went,
Or followed the track that they flew in,
For that Continent
Hadn't been given a name.
They ran thirty degrees,
From Torres Straits to the Leeuwin
(Look at the Atlas, please),
And they ran back as they came.

S'posing you could trot
From Adelaide to the Pacific,
For an afternoon's run—
Half what these gentlemen did—
You would feel rather hot,
But your legs would develop terrific—
Yes, my importunate son,
You'd be a Marvelous Kid!

The Tales of the Arabian Nights is a collection of fairy tales from Middle and Far Eastern countries. These stories were told through the years by people from Persia, Asia, and Arabia.

In "The Story of Ali Cogia, Merchant of Bagdad", Ali Cogia decides to make a pilgrimmage to Mecca. Before he leaves, he hides a thousand pieces of gold in a vase of olives and leaves the vase with a friend for safekeeping.

In "Aladdin and the Wonderful Lamp", Aladdin meets a powerful genie who lives inside a lamp. The genie helps him outsmart an evil magician, obtain many wonderful things, and pursue a beautiful princess.

The Tales of the Arabian Nights

AS RETOLD BY ANDREW LANG

THE STORY OF ALI COGIA, MERCHANT OF BAGDAD

After some thought, Ali Cogia hit upon a plan which seemed a safe one. He took a large vase, and placing the money in the bottom of it, filled up the rest with olives. After corking the vase tightly down, he carried it to one of his friends, a merchant like himself, and said to him: "My brother, you have probably heard that I am starting with a caravan in a few days for Mecca. I have come to ask whether you would do me the favor to keep this vase of olives for me until I come back?"

The merchant replied readily, "Look, this is the key of my shop: take it, and put the vase wherever you like. I promise that you shall find it in the same place on your return."

A few days later, Ali Cogia mounted the camel that he had laden with merchandise, joined the

caravan, and arrived in due time at Mecca. Like the other pilgrims he visited the sacred Mosque, and after all his religious duties were performed, he set out his goods to the best advantage, hoping to gain some customers among the passers-by.

Very soon two merchants stopped before the pile, and when they had turned it over, one said to the other: "If this man was wise he would take these things to Cairo, where he would get a much better price than he is likely to do here."

Ali Cogia heard the words, and lost no time in following the advice. He packed up his wares, and instead of returning to Bagdad, joined a caravan that was going to Cairo. The results of the journey gladdened his heart. He sold off everything almost directly, and bought a stock of Egyptian curiosities, which he intended selling at Damascus; but as the caravan with which he would have to travel would not be starting for another six weeks, he took advantage of the delay to visit the Pyramids, and some of the cities along the banks of the Nile.

Now the attractions of Damascus so fascinated the worthy Ali, that he could hardly tear himself away, but at length he remembered that he had a home in Bagdad, meaning to return by way of Aleppo, and after he had crossed the Euphrates, to follow the course of the Tigris.

But when he reached Mossoul, Ali had made such friends with some Persian merchants, that they persuaded him to accompany them to their native land, and even as far as India, and as it came to pass that seven years had slipped by since he had left Bagdad, and during all that time the friend with whom he had left the vase of olives had never once thought of him or of it. In fact, it was only a month before Ali Cogia's actual return that the affair came into his head at all, owing to his wife's remarking one day, that it was a long time since she had eaten any olives, and would like some.

"That reminds me," said the husband, "that before Ali Cogia went to Mecca seven years ago, he left a vase of olives in my care. But really by this time he must be dead, and there is no reason we should not eat the olives if we like. Give me a light, and I will fetch them and see how they taste."

"My husband," answered the wife, "beware, I pray, of your doing anything so base! Supposing seven years have passed without any news of Ali Cogia, he need not be dead for all that, and may come back any day. How shameful it would be to have to confess that you had betrayed your trust and broken the seal of the vase! Pay no attention to my idle words, I really have no desire for olives now. And probably after all this while they are no longer good. I have a presentiment that Ali Cogia will return, and what will he think of you? Give it up, I entreat."

The merchant, however, refused to listen to her advice, sensible though it was. He took a light and a dish and went into his shop.

"If you will be so obstinate," said his wife, "I cannot help it; but do not blame me if it turns out ill."

When the merchant opened the vase he found the topmost olives were rotten, and in order to see if the under ones were in better condition he shook some out into the dish. As they fell out a few gold pieces fell out too.

The sight of the money roused all the merchant's greed. He looked into the vase, and saw that all the bottom was filled with gold. He then replaced the olives and returned to his wife.

"My wife," he said, as he entered the room, "you were quite right; the olives are rotten, and I have recorked the vase so well that Ali Cogia will never know it has been touched."

"You would have done better to believe me," replied the wife. "I trust that no harm will come of it."

These words made no more impression on the merchant than the others had done; and he spent the whole night in wondering how he could manage to keep the gold

if Ali Cogia should come back and claim his vase. Very early next morning he went out and bought fresh new olives; he then threw away the old ones, took out the gold and hid it, and filled up the vase with the olives he had bought. This done he recorked the vase and put it in the same place where it had been left by Ali Cogia.

A month later Ali Cogia re-entered Bagdad, and as his house was still let he went to an inn; and the following day set out to see his friend the merchant, who received him with open arms and many expressions of surprise. After a few moments given to inquiries Ali Cogia begged the merchant to hand him over the vase that he had taken care of for so long.

"Oh certainly," said he, "I am only glad I could be of use to you in the matter. Here is the key to my shop; you will find the vase in the place where you put it."

Ali Cogia fetched his vase and carried it to his room at the inn, where he opened it. He thrust down his hand, but could feel no money; still he was persuaded it must be there. So he got some plates and vessels from his travelling kit and emptied out the olives. To no purpose. The gold was not there. The poor man was dumb with horror, then, lifting up his hands, he exclaimed, "Can my old friend really have committed such a crime?"

In great haste he went back to the house of the merchant. "My friend," he cried, "you will be astonished to see me again, but I can find nowhere in this vase a thousand pieces of gold that I placed in the bottom under the olives. Perhaps you may have taken a loan of them for your business purposes; if that is so you are most welcome. I will only ask you to give me a receipt, and you can pay the money at your leisure."

The merchant, who had expected something of the sort, had his reply all ready. "Ali Cogia," he said, "when you brought me the vase of olives did I ever touch it? I gave you the key to my shop and you put it yourself where you liked, and did you not find it in exactly the same spot and in the same state? If you placed any gold in it, it must be there still. I know nothing about that; you only told me there were olives. You can believe me or not, but I have not laid a finger on the vase."

Ali Cogia still tried every means to persuade the merchant to admit the truth. "I love peace," he said, "and shall deeply regret having to resort to harsh measures. Once more, think of your reputation. I shall be in despair if you oblige me to call in the aid of the law."

"Ali Cogia," answered the merchant, "you allow that it was a vase of olives you placed in my charge. You fetched it and removed it yourself, and now you tell me it contained a thousand pieces of gold, and that I must restore them to you! Did you ever say anything about them before? Why, I did not even know that the vase had olives in it! You never showed them to me. I wonder you have not demanded pearls or diamonds. Retire, I pray you, lest a crowd should gather in front of my shop."

By this time not only the casual passers-by, but also the neighboring merchants, were standing round, listening to the dispute, and trying every now and then to smoothe matters between them. But at the merchant's last words Ali Cogia resolved to lay the cause of the quarrel before them, and told them the whole story. They heard him to the end, and inquired of the merchant what he had to say.

The accused man admitted that he had kept Ali Cogia's vase in his shop; but he denied having touched it, and swore that as to what it contained he only knew what Ali Cogia had told him, and called them all to witness the insult that had been put upon him.

"You have brought it on yourself," said Ali Cogia, taking him by the arm, "and as you appeal to the law, the law you shall have it! Let us see if you will dare to repeat your story before the Cadi."

Now as a good Mussulman the merchant was forbidden to refuse this choice of a judge, so he accepted the test, and said to Ali Cogia, "Very well; I should like nothing better. We shall soon see which of us is in the right."

So the two men presented themselves before the Cadi, and Ali Cogia again repeated his tale. The Cadi asked what witnesses he had. Ali Cogia replied that he had not taken this precaution, as he had considered the man his friend, and up to that time had always found him honest.

The merchant, on his side, stuck to his story, and offered to swear solemnly that not only had he never stolen the thousand gold pieces, but that he did not even know they were there. The Cadi allowed him to take the oath, and pronounced him innocent.

Ali Cogia, furious at having to suffer such a loss, protested against the verdict, declaring that he would appeal to the Caliph, Haroun-al-Raschid, himself. But the Cadi paid no attention to his threats, and was quite satisfied that he had done what was right.

Judgment being given the merchant returned home triumphant, and Ali Cogia went back to his inn to draw up a petition to the Caliph. The next morning he placed himself on the road along which the Caliph must pass after midday prayer, and stretched out his petition to the officer who walked before the Caliph, whose duty it was to collect such things, and on entering the palace to hand them to his master. There Haroun-al-Raschid studied them carefully.

Knowing this custom, Ali Cogia followed the Caliph into the public hall of the palace, and waited the result. After some time the officer appeared, and told him that the Caliph had read his petition, and had appointed an hour the next morning to give him audience. He then inquired the merchant's address, so that he might be summoned to attend also.

That very evening, the Caliph, with his grand-vizir Giafar, and Mesrour, chief of the eunuchs, all three disguised, as was their habit, went out to take a stroll through the town.

Going down one street, the Caliph's attention was attracted by a noise, and looking through a door which opened into a court he perceived 10 or 12 children, playing in the moonlight. He hid himself in a dark corner, and watched them.

"Let us play at being the Cadi," said the brightest and quickest of them all; "I will be the Cadi. Bring before me Ali Cogia, and the merchant who robbed him of the thousand pieces of gold."

The boy's words recalled to the Caliph the petition he had read that morning, and he waited with interest to see what the children would do.

The proposal was hailed with joy by the other children, who had heard a great deal of talk about the matter, and they quickly settled the part each one was to play. The Cadi took his seat gravely, and an officer introduced first Ali Cogia, the plaintiff, and then the merchant who was the defendant.

Ali Cogia made a low bow, and pleaded his cause point by point; concluding by imploring the Cadi not to inflict on him such a heavy loss.

The Cadi having heard his case, turned to the merchant, and inquired why he had not repaid Ali Cogia the sum in question.

The false merchant repeated the reasons that the real merchant had given to the Cadi of Bagdad, and also offered to swear that he had told the truth.

"Stop a moment!" said the little Cadi, "before we come to oaths, I should like to examine the vase with the olives. Ali Cogia," he added, "have you got the vase with you?" and finding he had not, the Cadi continued, "go and get it and bring it to me."

So Ali Cogia disappeared for an instant, and then pretended to lay a vase at the feet of the Cadi, declaring it was his vase, which he had given to the accused for safe custody; and in order to be quite correct, the Cadi asked the merchant if he recognized it as the same vase. By his silence the merchant admitted the fact, and the Cadi then commanded to have the vase opened. Ali Cogia made a movement as if he was taking off the lid, and the little Cadi on his part made a pretense of peering into the vase.

"What beautiful olives!" he said, "I should like to taste one," and pretending to put one in his mouth, he added, "they are excellent!"

"But," he went on, "it seems to me odd that olives seven years old should be as good as that! Send for some dealers in olives, and let us hear what they say!"

Two children were presented to him as olive merchants, and the Cadi addressed them. "Tell me," he said, "how long can olives be kept so as to be pleasant eating?"

"My lord," replied the merchants, "however much care is taken to preserve them, they never last beyond the third year. They lose both taste and color, and are only fit to be thrown away."

"If that is so," answered the little Cadi, "examine this vase, and tell me how long the olives have been in it."

The olive merchants pretended to examine the olives and taste them; then reported to the Cadi that they were fresh and good.

"You are mistaken," said he, "Ali Cogia declares he put them in that vase seven years ago."

"My lord," returned the olive merchants, "we can assure you that the olives are those of the present year. And if you consult all the merchants in Bagdad you will not find one to give a contrary opinion."

The accused merchant opened his mouth as if to protest, but the Cadi gave him no time. "Be silent," he said, "you are a thief. Take him away and hang him." So the game ended, the children clapping their hands in applause, and leading the criminal away to be hanged.

ALADDIN AND THE WONDERFUL LAMP

There once lived a poor tailor who had a son called Aladdin, a careless, idle boy who would do nothing but play all day long in the streets with little idle boys like himself. This so grieved the father that he died; yet, in spite of his mother's tears and prayers, Aladdin did not mend his ways. One day, when he was playing in the streets as usual, a stranger asked him his age, and if he were not the son of Mustapha the tailor.

"I am, sir," replied Aladdin; "but he died a long while ago."

On this the stranger, who was a famous African magician, fell on his neck and kissed him, saying: "I am your uncle, and knew you from your likeness to my brother. Go to your mother and tell her I am coming."

Aladdin ran home and told his mother of his newly found uncle.

"Indeed, child," she said, "your father had a brother, but I always thought he was dead."

However, she prepared supper, and bade Aladdin seek his uncle, who came laden with wine and fruit. He presently fell down and kissed the place where Mustapha used to sit, bidding Aladdin's mother not to be surprised at not having seen him before, as he had been 40 years out of the country. He then turned to Aladdin, and asked him his trade, at which the boy hung his head, while his mother burst into tears. On learning that Aladdin was idle and would learn no trade, he offered to take a shop for him and stock it with merchandise. Next day he bought Aladdin a fine suit of clothes, and took him all over the city, showing him the sights, and brought him home at nightfall to his mother, who was overjoyed to see her son so fine.

Next day the magician led Aladdin into some beautiful gardens a long way outside the city gates. They sat down by a fountain, and the magician pulled a cake from his girdle, which he divided between them. They then journeyed onward till they almost reached the mountains. Aladdin was so tired that he begged to go back, but the magician beguiled him with pleasant stories, and led him on in spite of himself.

At last they came to two mountains divided by a narrow valley.

"We will go no farther," said the false uncle. "I will show you something wonderful; only do you gather up sticks while I kindle a fire."

When it was lit the magician threw on it a powder he had about him, at the same time saying some magical words. The earth trembled a little and opened in front of them, disclosing a square, flat stone with a brass ring in the middle to raise it by. Aladdin tried to run away, but the magician caught him and gave him a blow that knocked him down.

"What have I done, uncle?" he said piteously; whereupon the magician said more kindly: "Fear nothing, but obey me. Beneath this stone lies a treasure which is to be yours, and no one else may touch it, so you must do exactly as I tell you."

At the word treasure, Aladdin forgot his fears, and grasped the ring as he was told, saying the names of his father and grandfather. The stone came up quite easily and some steps appeared.

"Go down," said the magician; "at the foot of those steps you will find an open door leading into three large halls. Tuck up your gown and go through them without touching anything, or you will die instantly. These halls lead into a garden of fine fruit trees. Walk on till you come to a niche in a terrace where stands a lighted lamp. Pour out the oil it contains and bring it to me."

He drew a ring from his finger and gave it to Aladdin, bidding him prosper.

Aladdin found everything as the magician had said, gathered some fruit off the trees, and, having got the lamp, arrived at the mouth of the cave. The magician cried out in a great hurry:

"Make haste and give me the lamp." This Aladdin refused to do until he was out of the cave. The magician flew into a terrible passion, and throwing some more powder on the fire, he said something, and the stone rolled back into its place, trapping Aladdin inside.

The magician left Persia forever, which plainly showed that he was no uncle of Aladdin's, but a cunning magician who had read in his magic books of a wonderful lamp, which would make him the most powerful man in the world. Though he alone knew where to find it, he could only receive it from the hand of another. He had picked out the foolish Aladdin for the purpose, intending to get the lamp and kill him afterward.

For two days Aladdin remained in the dark, crying and lamenting. At last he clasped his hands in prayer, and in so doing rubbed the ring, which the magician had forgotten to take from him. Immediately an enormous and frightful genie rose out of the earth, saying: "What wouldst thou with me? I am the Slave of the Ring, and will obey thee in all things."

Aladdin fearlessly replied: "Deliver me from this place!" Whereupon the earth opened, and he found himself outside. As soon as his eyes could bear the light he went home, but fainted on the threshold. When he came to himself he told his mother what had passed, and showed her the lamp and the fruits he had gathered in the garden, which were in

reality precious stone. He then asked for some food.

"Alas! child," she said, "I have nothing in the house, but I have spun a little cotton and will go and sell it."

Aladdin bade her keep her cotton, for he would sell the lamp instead. As it was very dirty she began to rub it, that it might fetch a higher price. Instantly a hideous genie appeared, and asked what she would have. She fainted away, but Aladdin, snatching the lamp, said boldly: "Fetch me something to eat!"

The genie returned with a silver bowl, twelve silver plates containing rich meats, two silver cups, and two bottles of wine. Aladdin's mother, when she came to herself, said: "Whence comes this splendid feast?"

"Ask not, but eat," replied Aladdin.

So they sat at breakfast till it was dinner-time, and Aladdin told his mother about the lamp. She begged him to sell it, and have nothing to do with devils.

"No," said Aladdin, "since chance has made us aware of its virtues, we will use it and the ring likewise, which I shall always wear on my finger." When they had eaten all the genie had brought, Aladdin sold one of the silver plates, and so on till none were left. He then had recourse to the genie, who gave him another set of plates, and thus they lived for many years.

One day Aladdin heard an order from the Sultan, proclaiming that everyone was to stay at home and close his shutters while the princess, his daughter, went to and from the bath. Aladdin was seized by a desire to see her face, which was very difficult, as she always went veiled. He hid himself behind the door of the bath, and peeped through a chink. The princess lifted her veil as she went in, and looked so beautiful that Aladdin fell in love with her at first sight. He went home so changed that his mother was frightened. He told her he loved the princess so deeply that he could not live without her, and meant to ask her in marriage of her father. His mother, on hearing this, burst out laughing, but Aladdin at last prevailed upon her to go before the Sultan and carry his request. She fetched a napkin and laid in it the magic fruits from the enchanted garden, which sparkled and shone like the most beautiful jewels. She took these with her to please the Sultan, and set out, trusting in the lamp. The grand-vizir and the lords of council had just gone in as she entered the hall and placed herself in front of the Sultan. He, however, took no notice of her. She went every day for a week, and stood in the same place.

When the council broke up on the sixth day, the Sultan said to his vizir: "I see a certain woman in the audience-chamber every day carrying something in a napkin. Call her next time, that I may find out what she wants."

Next day, at a sign from the vizir, she went up to the foot of the throne, and remained kneeling till the Sultan said to her: "Rise, good woman, and tell me what you want."

She hesitated, so the Sultan sent away all but the vizir, and bade her speak freely, promising to forgive her beforehand for anything she might say. She then told him of her son's violent love for the princess.

"I prayed him to forget her," she said, "but in vain; he threatened to do some desperate deed if I refused to go and ask your Majesty for the hand of the princess. Now I pray you to forgive not me alone, but my son Aladdin."

The sultan asked her kindly what she had in the napkin, whereupon she unfolded the jewels and presented them.

He was thunderstruck, and turning to the vizir said: "What sayest thou? Ought I not to bestow the princess on one who values her at such a price?"

The vizir, who wanted her for his own son, begged the Sultan to withold her for three months, in the course of which he hoped his son would contrive to make him a richer present. The Sultan granted this, and told Aladdin's mother that, though he consented to the marriage, she must not appear before him again for three months.

Aladdin waited patiently for nearly three months, but after two had elapsed, his mother, going into the city to buy oil, found everyone rejoicing, and asked what was going on.

"Do you not know," was the answer, "that the son of the grand-vizir is to marry the Sultan's daughter tonight?"

Breathless, she ran and told Aladdin, who was overwhelmed at first, but presently bethought him of the lamp. He rubbed it, and the genie appeared, saying: "What is thy will?"

Aladdin replied: "The Sultan, as thou knowest, has broken his promise to me, and the vizir's son is to have the princess. My command is that tonight you bring hither the bride and bridegroom."

"Master, I obey," said the genie.

Aladdin then went to his chamber, where, sure enough, at midnight the genie transported the bed containing the vizir's son and the princess.

"Take this new-married man," he said, "and put him outside in the cold, and return at daybreak."

Whereupon the genie took the vizir's son out of bed, leaving Aladdin with the princess.

"Fear nothing," Aladdin said to her; "you are my wife, promised to me by your unjust father, and no harm shall come to you."

The Little Prince tells the story of a pilot's encounter with a young boy who has left his planet in search of companionship. Before meeting up with a Pilot, the little prince has a series of meetings with other people and animals. Here is his meeting with a fox, who is also in search of friendship.

The Little Prince

ANTOINE DE ST. EXUPÉRY

It was then that the fox appeared.

"Good morning," said the fox.

"Good morning," the little prince responded politely, although when he turned around he saw nothing.

"I am right here," the voice said, "under the apple tree."

"Who are you?" asked the little prince, and added, "You are very pretty to look at."

"I am a fox," the fox said.

"Come and play with me," proposed the little prince. "I am so unhappy."

"I cannot play with you," the fox said. "I am not tamed."

"Ah! Please excuse me," said the little prince. But, after some thought, he added: "What does that mean—'tame'?"

"You do not live here," said the fox. "What is it that you are looking for?"

"I am looking for men," said the little prince. "What does that mean—'tame'?"

"Men," said the fox. "They have guns, and they hunt. It is very

disturbing. They also raise chickens. These are their only interests. Are you looking for chickens?"

"No," said the little prince. I am looking for friends. What does that mean—'tame'?"

"It is an act too often neglected," said the fox. "It means to establish ties."

" 'To establish ties'?"

"Just that," said the fox. "To me, you are still nothing more than a little boy who is just like a hundred thousand other little boys. And I have no need of you. And you, on your part, have no need of me. To you I am nothing more than a fox like a hundred other foxes. But if you tame me, than we shall need each other. To me, you will be unique in all the world. To you I shall be unique in all the world . . ."

"I am beginning to understand," said the little prince. "There is a flower . . . I think that she has tamed me . . ."

"It is possible," said the fox. "On the Earth one sees all sorts of things."

"Oh, but this is not on the Earth!" said the little prince.

The fox seemed perplexed, and very curious.

"On another planet?"

"Yes."

"Are there hunters on that planet?"

"No."

"Ah, that is interesting! Are there chickens?"

"No."

"Nothing is perfect," sighed the fox.

But he came back to his idea.

"My life is very monotonous," he said. "I hunt chickens; men hunt me. All the chickens are just alike, and all the men are just alike. And, in consequence, I am a little bored. But if you tame me, it will be as if the sun came to shine on my life. I shall know the sound of a step that will be different from all others. Other steps send me hurrying back underneath the ground. Yours will call me, like music, out of my burrow. And then look: you see the grain fields down yonder? I do not eat bread. Wheat is of no use to me. The wheat fields have nothing to say to me. And that is sad. But you have hair that is the color of gold. Think how wonderful that will be when you have tamed me! The grain, which is golden, will bring me back to the thought of you. And I shall love to listen to the wind in the wheat . . ."

The fox gazed at the little prince for a long time.

"Please—tame me!" he said.

"I want to, very much," the little prince replied. "But I have not much time. I have friends to discover, and a great many things to understand."

"One only understands the things that one tames," said the fox. "Men have no more time to understand anything. They buy things all ready-made at the shops. But there is no shop anywhere where one can buy friendship and so men have no friends any more. If you want a friend, tame me. . . ."

"What must I do, to tame you?" asked the little prince.

"You must be very patient," replied the fox. "First you will sit down at a little distance

from me like that in the grass. I shall look at you out of the corner of my eye, and you will say nothing. Words are the source of misunderstandings. But you will sit a little closer to me, every day . . ."

The next day the little prince came back.

"It would have been better to come back at the same hour," said the fox. "If, for example, you come at four o'clock in the afternoon, then at three o'clock I shall begin to be happy. I shall feel happier and happier as the hour advances. At four o'clock, I shall already be worrying and jumping about. I shall show you how happy I am! But if you come at just any time, I shall never know at what hour my heart is to be ready to greet you . . . One must observe the proper rites . . ."

"What is a rite?" asked the little prince.

"Those also are actions too often neglected," said the fox. "They are what make one day different from other days, one hour from other hours. There is a rite, for example, among my hunters. Every Thursday they dance with the village girls. So Thursday is a wonderful day for me! I can take a walk as far as the vineyards. But if the hunters danced at just any time, every day would be like every other day and I should never have any vacation at all."

So the little prince tamed the fox. And when the hour of his departure drew near—

"Ah," said the fox, "I shall cry."

"It is your own fault," said the little prince. "I never wished you any sort of harm; but you wanted me to tame you. . . ."

"Yes, that is so," said the fox.

"But now you are going to cry!" said the little prince.

"Yes, that is so," said the fox.

"Then it has done you no good at all!"

"It has done me good," said the fox, "because of the color of the wheat fields." And then he added: "Go and look again at the roses. You will understand now that yours is unique in all the world. Then come back to say good-bye to me, and I will make a present of a secret."

The little prince went away, to look again at the roses.

"You are not at all like my rose," he said. "As yet you are nothing. No one has tamed you, and you have tamed no one. You are like my fox when I first knew him. He was only a fox, like a hundred thousand other foxes. But I have made him my friend, and now he is unique in all the world."

And the roses were very much embarrassed.

"You are beautiful, but you are empty," he went on. "One could not die for you. To be sure an ordinary passerby would think that my rose looked just like you the rose that belongs to me. But in herself alone she is more important than all the hundreds of other roses: because it is she that I have put under the glass globe; because it is for her that I have killed the caterpillar (except the two or three that we saved to become butterflies); because it is she that I have listened to, when she grumbled, or boasted, or even sometimes when she said nothing. Because she is my rose."

And he went back to meet the fox.

"Good-bye," he said.

"Good-bye," said the fox. "And now here is my secret, a very simple secret: It is only with the heart that one can see rightly; what is essential is invisible to the eye."

"What is essential is invisible to the eye," the little prince repeated, so that he would be sure to remember.

"It is the time you have wasted for your rose that makes your rose so important."

"It is the time I have wasted for my rose—" said the little prince, so that he would be sure to remember.

"Men have forgotten this truth," said the fox. "But you must not forget it. You become responsible forever, for what you have tamed. You are responsible for your rose . . ."

"I am responsible for my rose," the little prince repeated, so that he would be sure to remember.

One of the best-known children's stories, this is a tale of two children whose stepmother contrives to lose them in the forest so that she and her husband have enough food to eat. Once lost, Hansel and Gretel stumble hungrily upon a house made of bread and cakes. But the house is really a trap set by an old witch who intends to cook and eat the children. Using ingenious ploys, the children forestall the witch's evil plans and eventually kill her. Hauling away as much of the witch's treasure as they can carry, the children find the way home to their old guilty father, who rejoices at their return.

Hansel and Gretel

JACOB GRIMM AND
WILHELM GRIMM

Once upon a time there dwelt on the outskirts of a large forest a poor woodcutter with his wife and two children; the boy was called Hansel and the girl Gretel. He had always had little enough to live on, and once, when there was a great famine in the land, he couldn't even provide them with daily bread. One night, as he was tossing about in bed, full of cares and worry, he sighed and said to his wife: "What's to become of us? How are we to support our poor children, now that we have nothing for ourselves?"

"I'll tell you what, husband," answered the woman; "early tomorrow morning we'll take the children to the thickest part of the wood; there we shall light a fire for them and give them a piece of bread; and then we'll go on to our work and leave them alone. They won't be able to find their way home, and we shall thus be rid of them."

"No, wife," said her husband, "that I won't do; how could I find it in my heart to leave my children alone in the wood? The wild beasts would soon come and tear them to pieces."

"Oh! you fool," said she, "then we must all four

die of hunger, and you may just as well go and plane the boards for our coffins"; and she left him no peace till he consented.

"But I can't help feeling sorry for the poor children," added the husband.

The children, too, had not been able to sleep for hunger, and had heard what their stepmother had said to their father. Gretel wept bitterly and spoke to Hansel: "Now it's all up with us."

"No, no, Gretel," said Hansel, "don't fret yourself; I'll be able to find a way of escape, no fear."

And when the old people had fallen asleep he got up, slipped on his little coat, opened the back door, and stole out. The moon was shining clearly, and the white pebbles which lay in front of the house glittered like bits of silver. Hansel bent down and filled his pocket with as many of them as he could cram in. Then he went back and said to Gretel, "Be comforted, my dear little sister, and go to sleep: God will not desert us," and he lay down in bed again.

At daybreak, even before the sun was up, the woman came and woke the two children: "Get up, you lie-abeds, we're all going to the forest to fetch wood." She gave them each a bit of bread and spoke: "There's something for your luncheon, but don't you eat it up before, for it's all you'll get."

Gretel took the bread under her apron, as Hansel had the stones in his front pocket. Then they set out together on the way to the forest. After they had walked for a little, Hansel stood still and looked back at the house, and this maneuver he repeated again and again.

His father observed him and spoke: "Hansel, what are you gazing at there, and why do you always remain behind? Take care, and don't lose your footing."
"Oh! father," said Hansel, "I am looking at my white kitten, which is sitting on the roof, waving me a farewell."

The woman exclaimed: "What a donkey you are! That isn't your kitten, that's the morning sun sitting on the chimney."

But Hansel had not looked back at his kitten, but had always dropped one of the white pebbles out of his pocket on to the path.

When they had reached the middle of the forest the father said: "Now, children, go and fetch a lot of wood, and I'll light a fire that you mayn't feel cold." Hansel and Gretel heaped up brushwood till they had made a pile nearly the size of a small hill. The brushwood was set fire to, and when the flames leaped high the woman said: "Now lie down at the fire, children, and rest yourselves: we are going into the forest to cut down wood; when we've finished we'll come back and fetch you."

Hansel and Gretel sat down beside the fire, and at midday ate their bits of bread. They heard the strokes of the ax, so they thought their father was quite near. But it was no ax they heard, but a bough he had tied on to a dead tree, and that was blown about by the wind. And when they had sat for a long time their eyes closed with fatigue, and they fell fast asleep.

When they awoke at last it was pitch dark. Gretel began to cry and said: "How are we ever to get out of the wood?" But Hansel comforted her. "Wait a bit," he said, "till the moon is up, and then we'll find our way sure enough." And when the full moon had risen he took his sister by the hand and followed the pebbles, which shone like new three-penny bits and showed them the path. They walked all through the night, and at daybreak reached their father's house again.

They knocked at the door, and when the woman opened it she exclaimed: "You naughty children, what a time you've slept in the wood! We thought you were never going to come back."

But the father rejoiced, for his conscience had reproached him for leaving his children behind by themselves.

Not long afterward there was again great dearth in the land, and the children heard their mother address their father thus in bed one night: "Everything is eaten up once more; we have only half a loaf in the house, and when that's done it's all up with us. The children must be got rid of; we'll lead them deeper into the woods this time, so that they won't be able to find their way out again. There is no other way of saving ourselves."

The man's heart smote heavily, and he thought, "Surely it would be better to share the last bite with one's children!" But his wife wouldn't listen to his arguments, and did nothing but scold and reproach him. If a man yields once he's done for, and so, because he had given in the first time, he was forced to do so the second.

But the children were awake and had heard the conversation. When the old people were asleep Hansel got up and wanted to go out and pick up pebbles again, as he had one for the first time; but the woman had barred the door and Hansel couldn't get out. But he consoled his little sister and said: "Don't cry, Gretel, and sleep peacefully, for God is sure to help us."

At early dawn the woman came and made the children get up. They received their bit of bread, but it was even smaller than the time before. On the way to the wood Hansel crumbled it in his pocket, and every few minutes he stood still and dropped a crumb on the ground.

"Hansel, what are you stopping and looking about you for?" said the father.

"I'm looking back at my little pigeon, which is sitting on the roof waving me a farewell," answered Hansel.

"Fool!" said the wife; "that isn't your pigeon, it's the morning sun glittering on the chimney."

But Hansel gradually threw all his crumbs on to the path. The woman led the children still deeper into the forest, further than they had ever been in their lives before. Then a big fire was lit again, and the mother said: "Just sit down there, children, and if you're tired you can sleep a bit; we're going into the forest to cut down wood, and in the evening when we're finished we'll come back to fetch you."

At midday Gretel divided her bread with Hansel, for he had strewn his all along their path. Then they fell asleep, and evening passed away, but nobody came to the poor children. They didn't wake till it was pitch dark, and Hansel comforted his sister saying: "Only wait, Gretel, till the moon rises, then we shall see the breadcrumbs I scattered along the path; they will show us the way back to the house."

When the moon appeared they got up, but they found no crumbs, for thousands of birds that fly about the woods and fields had picked them up. "Never mind," said Hansel to Gretel; "you'll see we'll still find a way out"; but all the same they did not. They wandered about the whole night, and the next day, from morning till evening, but they could not find a path out of the wood. They were very hungry, too, for they had nothing to eat but a few berries they found growing on the ground. And at last they were so tired that their legs refused to carry them any longer, so they lay down under a tree and fell fast asleep.

On the third morning after they had left their father's house they set about their wandering again, but only got deeper and deeper into the wood, and now they felt that if help did not come to them soon they must perish. At midday they saw a beautiful little snow-white bird sitting on a branch, which sang so sweetly that they stopped still and listened to it. And when its song was finished it flapped its wings and flew on in front of them. They followed it and came to a little house, on the roof of which it perched; and when they came quite near they saw that the cottage was made of bread and roofed with cakes, while the window was made of transparent sugar. "Now we'll set to," said Hansel, "and have a regular blow out. I'll eat a bit of the roof, and you, Gretel, can eat some of the window, which you'll find a sweet morsel."

Hansel stretched up his hand and broke off a little bit of the roof to see what it was like, and Gretel went to the casement and began to nibble at it. Thereupon a shrill voice called out from the room inside:

> *Nibble, nibble, little mouse,*
> *Who's nibbling my house?'*

The children answered,

> *'Tis Heaven's own child,*
> *The tempest wild,*

and went on eating, without putting themselves about. Hansel, who thoroughly appreciated the roof, tore down a big bit of it, while Gretel pushed out a whole round window pane, and sat down the better to enjoy it. Suddenly the door opened and an ancient dame leaning on a staff hobbled out. Hansel and Gretel were so terrified that they let what they had in their hands fall. But the old woman shook her head and said: "Oh, ho! you dear children, who led you here? Just come in and stay with me: no ill shall befall you."

She took them both by the hand and led them in to the house, and laid a most sumptuous dinner before them—milk and sugared pancakes, with apples and nuts. After they had finished, two beautiful little white beds were prepared for them, and when Hansel and Gretel lay down in them they felt as if they had got into heaven.

The old woman appeared to be most friendly, but she was really an old witch who had waylaid the children, and had only built the little bread house in order to lure them in. When anyone came into her power she killed, cooked, and ate him, and held a regular feast-day for the occasion. Now, witches have red eyes and cannot see far, but, like beasts, they have a keen sense of smell and know when human beings pass by. When Hansel and Gretel fell into her hands she laughed maliciously and said jeeringly: "I've got them now; they shan't escape me."

Early in the morning, before the children were awake, she arose, and when she saw them both sleeping so peacefully, with their rosy round cheeks, she muttered to herself: "That'll

be a dainty bite." Then she seized Hansel with her bony hand and carried him into a little stable, and barred the door on him; he might scream as much as he liked, it did him no good.

Then she went to Gretel, shook her till she awoke, and cried: "Get up, you lazy-bones; fetch water and cook something for your brother. When he's fat I'll eat him up." Gretel began to cry bitterly, but it was of no use: she had to do what the wicked witch bade her.

So the best food was cooked for poor Hansel, but Gretel got nothing but crab-shells. Every morning the old woman hobbled out to the stable and cried: "Hansel, put out your finger, that I may feel if you are getting fat." But Hansel always stretched out a bone, and the old dame whose eyes were dim, couldn't see it, and thinking always it was Hansel's finger, wondered why he fattened so slowly. When four weeks passed and Hansel still remained thin, she lost patience and determined to wait no longer.

"Hi! Gretel," she called to the girl, "be quick and get some water. Hansel may be fat or thin, I'm going to kill him tomorrow and cook him." Oh! how the poor little sister sobbed as she carried the water, and how the tears rolled down her cheeks! "Kind Heaven help us now!" she cried; "if only the wild beasts in the wood had eaten us, then at least we should have died together."

"Just hold your peace," said the old hag; "it won't help you."

Early in the morning Gretel had to go out and hang up the kettle full of water and light the fire. "First we'll bake," said the old dame; "I've heated the oven already and kneaded the dough." She pushed Gretel out to the oven, from which fiery flames were already issuing.

"Creep in," said the witch, "and see if it's properly heated, so that we can shove in the bread." For when she had got Gretel in she meant to close the oven and let the girl bake, that she might eat her up too.

But Gretel perceived her intention and spoke: "I don't know how I'm going to do it; how do I get in?"

"You silly goose!" said the hag, "the opening is big enough; see, I could get in myself"; and she crawled toward it and poked her head into the oven. Then Gretel gave her a shove that sent her right in, shut the iron door, and drew the bolt. Gracious! how she yelled! it was quite horrible; but Gretel fled, and the wretched old woman was left to perish miserably.

Gretel flew straight to Hansel, opened the little stable door, and cried: "Hansel, we are free; the old witch is dead."

Then Hansel sprang like a bird out of the cage when the door is opened. How they rejoiced, and fell on each other's necks, and jumped for joy, and kissed one another! And as they had no longer any cause for fear, they went into the old hag's house, and there they found, in every corner of the room, boxes with pearls and precious stones.

"These are even better than pebbles," said Hansel, and crammed his pockets full of them; and Gretel said, "I too will bring something home"; and she filled her apron full.

"But now," said Hansel, "let's go and get well away from the witch's wood." When they had wandered about for some hours they came to a big lake. "We can't get over," said Hansel; "I see no bridge of any sort or kind."

Yes, and there's no ferryboat either," answered Gretel; "but look, there swims a white duck; if I ask her she'll help us over"; and she called out:

Here are two children, mournful very,
Seeing neither bridge nor ferry;
Take us upon your white back,
And row us over quack, quack!

The duck swam toward them, and Hansel got on her back and bade his little sister to sit beside him.

"No," answered Gretel, "we should be too heavy a load for the duck: she shall carry us across separately." The good bird did this, and when they were landed safely on the other side and had gone on for awhile, the wood became more and more familiar to them, and at length they saw their father's house in the distance. Then they set off to run, and bounding into the room fell on their father's neck.

The man had not passed a happy hour since he left them in the wood, but the woman had died. Gretel shook out her apron so that the pearls and precious stones rolled about the room, and Hansel threw down one handful after the other out of his pocket. Thus all their troubles were ended, and they all lived happily ever afterward.

This story of the vain and insecure emperor who was tricked by two swindlers into parading naked through the city is one of the world's truly timeless tales.

The Emperor's New Clothes

HANS CHRISTIAN ANDERSEN

Many years ago there was an Emperor who was so excessively fond of new clothes that he spent all his money on them. He cared nothing about his soldiers nor for the theatre, nor for driving in the woods except for the sake of showing off his new clothes. He had a costume for every hour in the day, and instead of saying, as one does about the other King or Emperor, "He is in his council chamber," here one always said, "The Emperor is in his dressing-room."

One day two swindlers came to visit the town. They gave themselves out as weavers, and said that they knew how to weave the most beautiful stuffs imaginable. Not only were the colors and patterns unusually fine, but the clothes that were made of the stuffs had the peculiar quality of becoming invisible to every person who was not fit for the office he held, or if he was impossibly dull.

"Those must be splendid clothes," thought the Emperor. "By wearing them I should be able to discover which men in my kingdom are unfitted for their posts. I shall distinguish the wise men from the fools. Yes, I certainly must order some of that stuff to be woven for me."

He paid the two swindlers a lot of money in advance, so that they might begin their work at once.

They did put up two looms and pretended to weave, but they had nothing whatever upon their shuttles. At the outset they asked for a quantity of the finest silk and the purest gold thread, all of which they put into their own bags while they worked away at the empty looms far into the night.

"I should like to know how those weavers are getting on with the stuff," thought the Emperor; but he felt a little queer when he reflected that anyone who was stupid or unfit for his post would not be able to see it. He certainly thought that he need have no fears for himself, but he still thought he would send somebody else first to see how it was getting on.

"I will send my faithful old minister to the weavers," thought the Emperor. "He will be best able to see how the stuff looks, for he is a clever man and no one fulfills his duties better than he does!"

So the good old minister went into the room where the two swindlers sat working at the empty loom.

"Heaven preserve us!" thought the old minister, opening his eyes very wide. "Why I can't see a thing!" But he took care not to say so.

Both the swindlers begged him to be good enough to step a little nearer, and asked if he did not think it a good pattern and beautiful coloring. They pointed to the empty loom, and the poor old minister stared and pretended to see cloth.

"Oh, it is beautiful! Quite charming!" said the old minister looking through his spectacles. "This pattern and these colors! I will certainly tell the Emperor that the stuff pleases me very much."

"We are delighted to hear you say so," said the swindlers, and then they named all the colors and described the peculiar pattern. The old minister paid great attention to what they said, so as to be able to repeat it when he got home to the Emperor.

Then the swindlers went on to demand more money, more silk, and more gold, to be able to proceed with the weaving; but they put it all in their own pockets—not a single strand was ever put into the loom, but they went on as before weaving into the empty loom.

The Emperor soon sent another faithful official to see the weavers, but he, too, could see nothing at all.

"Is this not a beautiful piece of stuff?" said both the swindlers, showing and explaining the beautiful patterns and colors which were not there to be seen.

"I know I am not a fool!" thought the man, "so it must be that I am unfit for my good post! It is very strange though! However one must not let it appear! So he praised the stuff he did not see, and assured him of his delight in the beautiful colors and the originality of the design. "It is absolutely charming!" he said to the Emperor. Everybody in the town was talking about this splendid stuff.

Now the Emperor thought he would like to see it while it was still on the loom. So he selected two faithful officials who had already seen the imaginary stuff, he went to visit the crafty imposters, who were working away as hard as ever they could at the empty loom.

"It is magnificent!" said both the honest officials. "Only see, your Majesty, what a design! What colors!" And they pointed to the empty loom, for they thought no doubt the others could see the stuff.

"What!" thought the Emperor; "I see nothing at all! This is terrible! Am I a fool? Am I not fit to be Emperor? Why, nothing worse could happen to me!"

"Oh, it is beautiful!" said the Emperor. "It has my highest approval!" and he nodded his satisfaction as he gazed at the empty loom. Nothing would induce him to say that he could not see anything.

The whole suite gazed, but saw nothing more than all the others. However, they all exclaimed with his Majesty, "It is very beautiful!" and they advised him to wear a suit made of this wonderful cloth on the occasion of a great procession which was just about to take place. "It is magnificent! Gorgeous! Excellent!" went from mouth to mouth; they were all equally delighted with it. The Emperor gave each of the rogues the title of "Gentlemen weavers."

The swindlers sat up the whole night, before the day on which the procession was to take place, cutting the air with a huge pair of scissors, and they stitched away with needles without any thread in them. At last they said: "Now the Emperor's new clothes are ready!"

The Emperor, with his grandest courtiers, went to them himself, and both the swindlers raised one arm in the air, as if they were holding something, and said: "See, these are the trousers, this is the coat, and here is the mantle!" and so on. "It is as light as a spider's web. One might think one had nothing on, but that is the very beauty of it!"

"Yes!" said all the courtiers, but they could not see anything, for there was nothing to see.

"Will your imperial Majesty be graciously pleased to take off your clothes," said the imposters, "so that we may put on the new ones, along here before the great mirror."

The Emperor took off all his clothes, and the imposters pretended to give him one article of dress after the other, of the new ones which they pretended to make. They pretended to fasten something round his waist and to tie on something; this was the train, and the Emperor turned round and round in front of the mirror.

"How well his Majesty looks in his new clothes! How becoming they are! They are the most gorgeous robes!"

"The canopy is waiting outside which is to be carried over your Majesty in the procession," said the master of ceremonies.

"Well I am quite ready," said the Emperor. "Don't the clothes fit well?" And then he turned around again in front of the mirror, so that he should seem to be looking at his grand things.

The chamberlains who were to carry the train stopped and pretended to lift it from the ground with both hands, and they walked along with their hands in the air. They dared not let it appear that they could not see anything.

Then the Emperor walked along in the procession under the gorgeous canopy, and everybody in the streets and at the windows exclaimed, "How beautiful the Emperor's new clothes are! What a splendid new train! and they fit to perfection!" Nobody would let it appear that he could see nothing, for then he would not be fit for his post, or else he was a fool.

None of the Emperor's clothes had been so successful before.

"But he has got nothing on," said a little child.

"Oh, listen to the innocent," said its father; and one person whispered to the other what the child had said. "He has nothing on; a child says he has nothing on!"

"But he has nothing on!" at last cried all the people.

The Emperor writhed, for he knew it was true, but he thought, "The procession must go on now," so held himself stiffer than ever, and the chamberlains held up the invisible train.

Wendy Darling and her brothers, John and Michael get an unexpected visit one night from the captain of the lost boys, Peter Pan and his fairy Tinker Bell. Peter Pan tells Wendy about his home in Neverland and she teaches him what a kiss is.

Peter Pan

J. M. BARRIE

CHAPTER 3
COME AWAY, COME AWAY!

A moment after the fairy's entrance the window was blown open by the breathing of the little stars, and Peter dropped in. He had carried Tinker Bell part of the way, and his hand was still messy with the fairy dust.

"Tinker Bell," he called softly, after making sure that the children were asleep, "Tink, where are you?" She was in a jug for the moment, and liking it extremely; she had never been in a jug before.

"Oh, do come out of that jug, and tell me, do you know where they put my shadow?"

The loveliest tinkle as of golden bells answered him. It is the fairy language. You ordinary children can never hear it, but if you were to hear it you would know that you had heard it once before.

Tink said that the shadow was in the big box. She meant the chest of drawers, and Peter jumped at the drawers, scattering their contents to the floor with both hands, as kings toss ha'pence to the crowd. In a moment he had recovered his shadow, and in his delight he forgot that he had shut Tinker Bell up in the drawer.

If he had thought at all, but I don't believe he ever thought, it was that he and his shadow, when brought near each other, would join like drops of water; and when they did not he was appalled. He tried to stick it on with soap from the bathroom, but that also failed. A shudder passed through Peter, and he sat on the floor and cried.

His sobs woke Wendy, and she sat up in bed. She was not alarmed to see a stranger crying on the nursery floor; she was only pleasantly interested.

"Boy," she said courteously, "why are you crying?"

Peter politefully bowed and she bowed back.

"What's your name?" he asked.

"Wendy Moira Angela Darling," she replied with some satisfaction. "What is your name?"

"Peter Pan."

She was already sure that he must be Peter, but it did seem a comparatively short name. "Is that all?"

"Yes," he said rather sharply. He felt for the first time that it was a shortish name.

"I'm so sorry," said Wendy Moira Angela.

"It doesn't matter," Peter gulped.

She asked where he lived.

"Second to the right," said Peter, "and then straight on till morning."

"What a funny address!"

Peter had a sinking feeling. For the first time he felt that perhaps it was a funny address. "No, it isn't," he said.

"I mean," Wendy said nicely, remembering that she was hostess, "is that what they put on the letters?"

He wished she had not mentioned letters.

"Don't get any letters," he said contemptuously.

"But your mother gets letters?"

"Don't have a mother," he said. Not only had he no mother, but he had not the slightest desire to have one. He thought them very overrated persons. Wendy, however, felt at once that she was in the presence of a tragedy.

"O Peter, no wonder you were crying," she said, and got out of bed and ran to him.

"I wasn't crying about mothers," he said rather indignantly. "I was crying because I can't get my shadow to stick on. Besides, I wasn't crying."

"It has come off?"

"Yes."

Then Wendy saw the shadow on the floor and felt sorry for Peter. He had been trying to stick it on with soap. How exactly like a boy!

Fortunately she knew at once what to do. "It must be sewn on," she said, just a little patronizingly.

"What's sewn?" he asked.

"You're dreadfully ignorant."

"No, I'm not."

But she was exulting in his ignorance. "I shall sew it on for you, my little man," she said, though he was as tall as herself; and she sewed the shadow on to Peter's foot.

"I daresay it will hurt a little," she warned him.

"Oh, I shan't cry," said Peter, and soon his shadow was behaving properly, though still a little creased.

"Perhaps I should have ironed it," Wendy said thoughtfully; but Peter, boylike, was indifferent to appearances, and he was now jumping about in the wildest glee. Alas, he had already forgotten that he owed his bliss to Wendy. He thought he had attached the shadow himself. "How clever I am," he crowed rapturously, "oh, the cleverness of me!"

It is humiliating to have to confess that this conceit of Peter was one of his most fascinating qualities. To put it with brutal frankness, there never was a cockier boy.

But for the moment Wendy was shocked. "You conceit," she exclaimed, with frightful sarcasm; "of course I did nothing!"

"You did a little," Peter said carelessly, and continued to dance.

"A little!" she replied with hauteur; "if I am no use I can at least withdraw"; and she sprang in the most dignified way into bed and covered her face with the blankets.

To induce her to look up pretended to be going away, and when this failed he sat on the end of the bed and tapped her gently with his foot. "Wendy," he said, "don't withdraw. I can't help crowing, Wendy, when I'm pleased with myself." Still she would not look up, though she was listening eagerly. "Wendy," he continued in a voice that no woman has ever yet been able to resist, "Wendy, one girl is more use than twenty boys."

Now Wendy was every inch a woman, though there were not very many inches, and she peeped out of the bedclothes.

"Do you really think so, Peter?"

"Yes, I do."

"I think it's perfectly sweet of you," she declared, "and I'll get up again"; and she sat with him on the side of the bed. She also said she would give him a kiss if he liked, but Peter did not know what she meant, and he held out his hand expectantly.

"Surely you know what a kiss is?" she asked aghast.

"I shall know when you give it to me," he replied stiffly; and not to hurt his feeling she gave him a thimble.

"Now," said he, "shall I give you a kiss?" and she replied with a slight primness, "If you please." She made herself rather cheap by inclining her face toward him, but he merely dropped an acorn button into her hand; so she slowly returned her face to where it had been before, and said nicely that she would wear his kiss on the chain round her neck. It was lucky that she did put it on that chain, for it was afterward to save her life.

When people in our set are introduced, it is customary for them to ask each other's age, and so Wendy, who always liked to do the correct thing, asked Peter how old he was. It was not really a happy question to ask him; it was like an examination paper that asks grammar, when what you want to be asked is Kings of England.

"I don't know," he replied uneasily, "but I am quite young." He really knew nothing about it; he had merely suspicions, but he said at a venture, "Wendy, I ran away the day I was born."

Wendy was quite surprised, but interested; and she indicated in the charming draw-ingroom manner, by a touch on her night-gown, that he could sit nearer her.

"It was because I heard father and mother," he explained in a low voice, "talking about what I was to be when I became a man." He was extraordinarily agitated now. "I don't want ever to be a man," he said with passion. "I want always to be a little boy and to have fun. So I ran away to Kensington Gardens and lived a long long time among the fairies."

Wendy had lived such a home life that to know fairies struck her as quite delightful. She poured out questions about them, to his surprise, for they were rather a nuisance to him, getting in his way, and so on, and indeed he sometimes had to give them a hiding.

Still, he liked them on the whole, and he told her about the beginnings of the fairies.

"You see, Wendy, when the first baby laughed for the first time, its laugh broke into a thousand pieces, and they all went skipping about, and that was the beginning of fairies."

Tedious talk this, but being a stay-at-home she liked it.

"And so," he went on good-naturedly, "there ought to be one fairy for every boy and girl."

"Ought to be? Isn't there?"

"No. You see children know such a lot now, they soon don't believe in fairies, and every time a child says, 'I don't believe in fairies,' there is a fairy somewhere that falls down dead."

Really, he thought they had now talked enough about fairies, and it struck him that Tinker Bell was keeping very quiet. "I can't think where she has gone to," he said, rising, and he called Tink by name. Wendy's heart went flutter with a sudden thrill.

"Peter," she cried, clutching him, "you don't mean to tell me that there is a fairy in this room!"

"She was here just now," he said a little impatiently. "You don't hear her, do you?" and they both listened.

"The only sound I hear," said Wendy, "is like a tinkle of bells."

"Well, that's Tink, that's the fairy language. I think I hear her too."

The sound came from the chest of drawers, and Peter made a merry face. No one could ever look quite so merry as Peter, and the loveliest of gurgles was his laugh. He had his first laugh still.

"Wendy," he whispered gleefully, "I do believe I shut her up in the drawer!"

He let poor Tink out of the drawer, and she flew about the nursery screaming with fury. "You shouldn't say such things," Peter retorted. "Of course I'm very sorry, but how could I know you were in the drawer?"

Wendy was not listening to him. "O Peter," she cried, "if she would only stand still and let me see her!"

"They hardly ever stand still," he said, but for one moment Wendy saw the romantic figure come to rest on the cuckoo clock. "O the lovely!" she cried, though Tink's face was still distorted with passion.

"Tink," said Peter amiably, "this lady says she wishes you were her fairy."

Tinker Bell answered insolently.

"What does she say, Peter?"

He had to translate. "She is not very polite. She says you are a great ugly girl, and that she is my fairy."

He tried to argue with Tink. "You know you can't be my fairy, Tink, because I am a gentleman and you are a lady."

To this Tink replied in these words, "you silly ass," and disappeared into the bathroom. "She is quite a common fairy," Peter explained apologetically; "she is called Tinker Bell because she mends the pots and kettles."

They were together in the armchair by this time, and Wendy plied him with more questions.

"If you don't live in Kensington Gardens now—"

"Sometimes I do still."

"But where do you live mostly now?"

"With the lost boys."

"Who are they?"

"They are the children who fall out of their perambulators when the nurse is looking the other way. If they are not claimed in seven days they are sent far away to the Neverland to defray expenses. I'm captain."

"What fun it must be!"

"Yes," said cunning Peter, "but we are rather lonely. You see we have no female companionship."

"Are none of the others girls?"

"Oh no; girls, you know, are much too clever to fall out of their prams."

This flattered Wendy immensely. "I think," she said, "it is perfectly lovely the way you talk about girls; John there just despises us."

For reply Peter rose and kicked John out of bed, blankets and all; one kick. This seemed to Wendy rather forward for a first meeting, and she told him with spirit that he was not captain in her house.

However, John continued to sleep so placidly on the floor that she allowed him to remain there. "And I know you meant to be kind," she said, relenting, "so you may give me a kiss."

For the moment she had forgotten his ignorance about kisses. "I thought you would want it back," he said a little bitterly, and offered to return her the thimble.

"Oh dear," said the nice Wendy, "I don't mean a kiss, I mean a thimble."

"What's that?"

"It's like this." She kissed him.

Cinderella lives with her stepmother and stepsisters who are rather unkind to her. One day, the King announces that his son will host a ball. The stepsisters begin their preparations, but Cinderella is told she is too homely to go to a ball. With the help of her dear godmother, however, all her dreams come true.

Cinderella, or, the Little Glass Slipper

CHARLES PERRAULT

Once there was a gentleman who married for his second wife the proudest and most haughty woman that was ever seen. She had by a former husband two daughters of her own humor, who were, indeed, exactly like her in all things. He had likewise, by his first wife, a young daughter, but of unparalleled goodness and sweetness of temper, which she took from her mother, who was the best creature in the world.

No sooner were the ceremonies of the wedding over but the mother-in-law began to show herself in her true colors. She could not bear the good qualities of this pretty girl, and the less because they made her own daughters appear the more odious. She employed her in the meanest work of the house: she scoured the dishes, tables, etc., and scrubbed madam's chamber and those of misses, her daughters; she lay up in a sorry garret, upon a wretched straw bed, while her sisters lay in fine rooms, with floors all inlaid, upon beds of the very

newest fashion, and where they had looking-glasses so large that they might see themselves at their full length from head to foot.

The poor girl bore all patiently and dared not to tell her father, who would have rattled her off; for his wife governed him entirely. When she had done her work she used to go into the chimney-corner and sit down among cinders and ashes, which made her commonly be called a cinder wench; but the youngest, who was not so rude and uncivil as the eldest, called her Cinderella. However, Cinderella, notwithstanding her mean apparel, was a hundred times handsomer than her sisters, though they were always dressed very richly.

It happened that the king's son gave a ball and invited all persons of fashion to it. Our young misses were also invited, for they cut a very grand figure among the quality. They were mightily delighted at this invitation, and wonderfully busy in choosing out such gowns, petticoats, and head-clothes as might become them. This was a new trouble to Cinderella, for it was she who ironed her sisters' linen and plaited their ruffles. They talked all day long of nothing but how they should be dressed.

"For my part," said the eldest, "I will wear my red velvet suit with French trimming."

"And I," said the youngest, "shall have my usual petticoat; but then, to make amends for that, I will put on my gold-flowered manteau and my diamond stomacher, which is far from being the most ordinary one in the world."

They sent for the best tire-woman they could get to make up their head-dresses and adjust their double pinners, and they had their red brushes and patches from Mademoiselle de la Poche.

Cinderella was likewise called up to them to be consulted in all these matters, for she had excellent notions and advised them always for the best, and offered her services to dress their heads, which they were very willing she should do. As she was doing this they said to her:

"Cinderella, would you not be glad to go to the ball?"

"Alas!" said she, "you only jeer me. It is not for such as I am to go thither."

"Thou art in the right of it," replied they. "It would make the people laugh to see a cinder wench at a ball."

Any one but Cinderella would have dressed their heads awry, but she was very good and dressed them perfectly well. They were almost two days without eating, so much they were transported with joy. They broke above a dozen of laces in trying to be laced up close, that they might have a fine slender shape, and they were continually at their looking-glass, at last the happy day came. The went to court, and Cinderella followed them with her eyes as long as she could, and when she had lost sight of them she fell a-crying.

Her godmother, who saw her all in tears, asked her what was the matter.

"I wish I could—I wish I could—"

She was not able to speak the rest, being interrupted by her tears and sobbing.

This godmother of hers, who was a fairy, said to her: "Thou wishest thou couldst go to the ball. Is it not so?"

"Y-es," cried Cinderella, with a great sigh.

"Well," said her godmother, "be but a good girl, and I will contrive that thou shalt go." Then she took her into her chamber and said to her: "Run into the garden and bring me a pumpkin."

Cinderella went immediately to gather the finest she could get, and brought it to her godmother, not being able to imagine how this pumpkin could make her go to the ball. Her godmother scooped out all the inside of it, having left nothing but the rind; which done, she struck it with her wand, and the pumpkin was instantly turned into a fine coach, gilded all over with gold.

She then went to look into her mouse-trap, where she found six mice, all alive, and ordered Cinderella to lift up a little the trap-door, when, giving each mouse as it went out a little tap with her wand, the mouse was that moment turned into a fine horse, which altogether made a very fine set of six horses of a beautiful mouse-colored dapple-gray. Being at a loss for a coachman, Cinderella said: "I will go and see if there is never a rat in the rat-trap—we may make a coachman of him."

"Thou art in the right," replied her godmother. "Go and look."

Cinderella brought the trap to her, and in it there were three huge rats. The fairy made choice of one of the three which had the largest beard, and having touched him with her wand he was turned into a fat, jolly coachman, who had the smartest whiskers ever beheld. After that she said "Go again into the garden, and you will find six lizards behind the watering-pot. Bring them to me."

She had no sooner done so but her godmother turned them into six footmen, who skipped up immediately behind the coach, with their liveries all bedaubed with gold and silver, and clung as close behind each other as if they had done nothing else their whole lives. The fairy then said to Cinderella:

"Well, you see here an equipage fit to go to the ball with. Are you not pleased with it?"

"Oh! yes," cried she; "but must I go thither as I am, in these nasty rags?"

Her godmother only just touched her with her wand, and at the same instant her clothes were turned into cloth-of-gold and silver, all beset with jewels. This done, she gave her a pair of glass slippers, the prettiest in the whole world. Being thus decked out, she got up into her coach; but her godmother, above all things, commanded her not to stay till after midnight, telling her at the same time that if she stayed one moment longer the coach would be a pumpkin again, her horses mice, her coachman a rat, her footmen lizards, and her clothes become just as they were before.

She promised her godmother she would not fail of leaving the ball before midnight, and then away she drives, scarce able to contain herself for joy. The king's son, who was told that a great princess, whom nobody knew, had come, ran out to receive her. He gave her his hand as she alighted out of the coach, and led her into the hall among all the company. There was immediately a profound silence, they left off dancing, and the violins ceased to play, so attentive was every one to contemplate the singular beauties of the unknown new-comer. Nothing was then heard but a confused noise of "Ha! how handsome she is! Ha! How handsome she is!"

The king himself, old as he was, could not help watching her and telling the queen softly that it was a long time since he had seen so beautiful and lovely a creature.

All the ladies were busied in considering her clothes and head-dress, that they might have some made next day after the same pattern, provided they could meet with such fine materials and as able hands to make them.

The king's son conducted her to the most honorable seat and afterward took her out to dance with him. She danced so very gracefully that they all more and more admired her. A fine collation was served up, whereof the young prince ate not a morsel, so intently was he busied in gazing on her.

She went and sat down by her sister, showing them a thousand civilities, giving them part of the oranges and citrons which the prince had presented her with, which very much surprised them, for they did not know her. While Cinderella was thus amusing her sisters, she heard the clock strike eleven and three-quarters, whereupon she immediately made a curtsey to the company and hastened away as fast as she could.

On arriving home, she ran to seek out her godmother, and after having thanked her she said she could not but heartily wish she might go next day to the ball, because the king's son had desired her to.

As she was eagerly telling her godmother what had passed at the ball her two sisters knocked at the door, which Cinderella ran and opened.

"How long you have stayed!" cried she, gaping, rubbing her eyes, and stretching herself as if she had been just waked out of her sleep. She had not, however, had any manner of inclination to sleep since they went from home. "If thou hadst been at the ball," said one of her sisters, "thou wouldst not have been tired with it. There came thither the finest princess, the most beautiful ever was seen with mortal eyes. She showed us a thousand civilities and gave us oranges and citrons."

Cinderella seemed very indifferent in the matter. Indeed, she asked them the name of that princess, but they told her they did not know it, and that the king's son was very uneasy on her account and would give all the world to know who she was. At this Cinderella, smiling, replied:

"She must, then, be very beautiful indeed. How happy you have been! Could not I see her? Ah! dear Miss Charlotte, do lend me your yellow suit of clothes which you wear every day."

"Ay, to be sure!" cried Miss Charlotte; "lend my clothes to such a dirty cinder wench as thou art! I should be a fool."

Cinderella expected well such answer and was very glad of the refusal, for she would have been sadly put to it if her sister had lent her what she asked for jestingly.

The next day the two sisters were at the ball, and so was Cinderella, but dressed more magnificently than before. The king's son was always by her and never ceased his compliments and kind speeches to her, to whom all this was so far from being tiresome that she quite forgot what her godmother had recommended to her, so that she at last counted the clock striking twelve when she took it to be no more than eleven. She then rose up and fled as nimble as a deer. The prince followed, but could not overtake her. She left behind one of her glass slippers, which the prince took up most carefully. She got home, but quite out of breath, and in her old clothes, having nothing left of all finery but one of the little slippers, fellow to that she dropped. The guards at the palace gate were asked if they had not seen a princess go out.

They said they had seen nobody go out but a young girl, very meanly dressed, and who had more of the air of a poor country wench than a gentlewoman.

When the two sisters returned from the ball Cinderella asked them if they had been well diverted and if the fine lady had been there.

They told her yes, but that she hurried away immediately when it struck twelve, and with so much haste that she dropped one of her little glass slippers, the prettiest in the world, which the king's son had taken up; that he had done nothing but look at her all the time at the ball, and that most certainly he was very much in love with the beautiful person who owned the glass slipper.

What they said was very true, for a few days after the king's son caused it to be proclaimed, by sound of trumpet, that he would marry her whose foot this slipper would just fit. They whom he employed began to try it upon the princesses, then the duchesses and all the court, but in vain. It was brought to the two sisters, who did all they possible could to thrust their foot into the slipper, but they could not make it fit. Cinderella, who saw all this and knew her slipper, said to them, laughing:

"Let me see if it will not fit me."

Her sisters burst out a-laughing and began to banter her. The gentleman who was sent to try the slipper looked earnestly at Cinderella, and finding her very handsome said it was but just that she should try, and that he had orders to let every one make trial.

He obliged Cinderella to sit down, and putting the slipper to her foot he found it went on very easily and fitted her as if it had been made of wax. The astonishment her two sisters were in was excessively great, but still abundantly greater when Cinderella pulled out of her pocket the other slipper and put it on her foot. Thereupon in came her godmother, who, having touched with her wand Cinderella's clothes, made them richer and more magnificent than any of those she had before.

And now her two sisters found her to be that fine, beautiful lady whom they had seen at the ball. They threw themselves at her feet to beg pardon for all the ill-treatment, and as she embraced them cried that she forgave them with all her heart and desired them always to love her.

She was conducted to the young prince, dressed as she was. He thought her more charming than ever and a few days after married her. Cinderella, who was no less good than beautiful, gave her two sisters lodgings in the palace, and that very same day matched them with two great lords of the court.

This is the story of a young princess who is cursed at her birth by an old fairy. The fairy declared that the princess would prick her finger on a spindle and fall into a deep slumber that could only be broken by a prince.

Sleeping Beauty in the Wood

CHARLES PERRAULT AND
MADAME D'AULNOY

Once upon a time there lived a king and queen who were grieved, more grieved than words can tell, because they had no children. They tried the waters of every country, made vows and pilgrimages, and did everything that could be done, but without result. At last, however, the queen found that her wishes were fulfilled, and in due course she gave birth to a daughter.

A grand christening was held, and all the fairies that could be found in the realm (they numbered seven in all) were invited to be godmothers to the little princess. This was done so that by means of the gifts which each in turn would bestow upon her (in accordance with the fairy custom of those days) the princess might be endowed with every imaginable perfection.

When the christening was held, all the company returned to the king's palace, where a great banquet was held in honor of the fairies. Places were laid for them in magnificent style, and before each was placed a solid gold casket containing a spoon, fork, and knife of fine gold, set with diamonds and rubies. But just as all were sitting down to table an aged fairy was seen to enter, whom no one had thought to invite—the reason being that for more than 50 years she had never quitted the tower in which she lived, and people had supposed her to be dead or bewitched.

By the king's orders a place was laid for her, but it was impossible to find her a golden casket like the others, for only seven had been made for the seven fairies. The old creature believed that she was intentionally slighted, and muttered threats between her teeth.

She was overheard by one of the young fairies, who was seated nearby. The latter, guessing that some mischievous gift might be bestowed upon the little princess, hid behind the tapestry as soon as the company left the table. Her intention was to be the last to speak, and so to have the power of counteracting, as far as possible, any evil which the old fairy might do.

Presently the fairies began to bestow their gifts upon the princess. The youngest ordained that she should be the most beautiful person in the world; the next, that she should have the temper of an angel; the third, that she should do everything with wonderful grace; the fourth, that she should dance to perfection; the fifth, that she should sing like a nightingale; and the sixth, that she should play every kind of music with the utmost skill.

It was now the turn of the aged fairy. Shaking her head, in token of spite rather than of infirmity, she declared that the princess should prick her hand with a spindle, and die of it. A shudder ran through the company at this terrible gift. All eyes were filled with tears.

But at this moment a young fairy stepped forth from behind the tapestry.

"Take comfort, your Majesties," she cried in a loud voice; "your daughter shall not die. My power, it is true, is not enough to undo all that my aged kinswoman has decreed: the princess will indeed prick her hand with a spindle. But instead of dying she shall merely fall into a profound slumber that will last a hundred years. At the end of that time a king's son shall come to awaken her."

The king, in an attempt to avert the unhappy doom pronounced by the old fairy, at once published an edict forbidding all persons, under pain of death, to use a spinning-wheel or keep a spindle in the house.

At the end of 15 or 16 years the king and queen happened one day to be away, on pleasure bent. The princess was running about the castle, and going upstairs from room to room she came at length to a garret at the top of a tower, where an old serving-woman sat alone with her distaff, spinning. This good woman had never heard speak of the king's proclamation forbidding the use of spinning-wheels.

"What are you doing, my good woman?" asked the princess.

"I am spinning, my pretty child," replied the dame, not knowing who she was.

"Oh, what fun!" rejoined the princess; "how do you do it? Let me try and see if I can do it equally well."

Partly because she was too hasty, partly because she was a little heedless, but also because the fairy decree had ordained it, no sooner had she seized the spindle than she pricked her hand and fell down in a swoon.

In great alarm the good dame cried out for help. People came running from every quarter to the princess. They threw water on her face, chafed her with their hands, and rubbed her temples with the royal essence of Hungary. But nothing would restore her.

Then the king, who had been brought upstairs by the commotion, remembered the fairy prophecy. Feeling certain that what had happened was inevitable, since the fairies had decreed it, he gave orders that the princess should be placed in the finest apartment in the palace, upon a bed embroidered in gold and silver.

You would have thought her an angel, so fair was she to behold. The trance had not taken away the lovely color of her complexion. Her cheeks were delicately flushed, her lips like coral. Her eyes, indeed, were closed, but her gentle breathing could be heard, and it was therefore plain that she was not dead. The king commanded that she should be left to sleep in peace until the hour of her awakening should come.

When the accident happened to the princess, the good fairy who had saved her life by condemning her to sleep a hundred years was in the kingdom of Mataquin, 12,000 leagues away. She was instantly warned of it, however, by a little dwarf who had a pair of seven-league boots, which are boots that enable one to cover seven leagues at a single step. The fairy set off at once, and within an hour her chariot of fire, drawn by dragons, was seen approaching.

The king handed her down from her chariot, and she approved of all that he had done. But being gifted with great powers of foresight, she bethought herself that when the princess came to be awakened, she would be much distressed to find herself all alone in the old castle. And this is what she did.

She touched with her wand everybody (except the king and queen) who was in the castle—governesses, maids of honor, ladies-in-waiting, gentlemen, officers, stewards, cooks,

scullions, errand boys, guards, porters, pages, footmen. She touched likewise all the horses in the stables, with their grooms, the big mastiffs in the courtyard, and little Puff, the pet dog of the princess, who was lying on the bed beside his mistress. The moment she had touched them they all fell asleep, to awaken only at the same moment as their mistress. Thus they would always be ready with their service whenever she should require it. The very spits before the fire, loaded with partridges and pheasants, subsided into slumber, and the fire as well. All was done in a moment, for the fairies do not take long over their work.

Then the king and queen kissed their dear child, without waking her, and left the castle. Proclamations were issued, forbidding any approach to it, but these warnings were not needed, for within a quarter of an hour there grew up all round the park so vast a quantity of trees big and small, with interlacing brambles and thorns, that neither man nor beast could penetrate them. The tops alone of the castle towers could be seen, and these only from a distance. Thus did the fairy's magic contrive that the princess, during all the time of her slumber, should have nought whatever to fear from prying eyes.

At the end of a hundred years the throne had passed to another family from that of the sleeping princess. One day the king's son chanced to go a-hunting that way, and seeing in the distance some towers in the midst of a large and dense forest, he asked what they were. His attendants told him in reply the various stories which they had heard. Some said there was an old castle haunted by ghosts, others that all the witches of the neighborhood held their revels there. The favorite tale was that in the castle lived an ogre, who carried thither all the children whom he could catch. There he dispensed with them at his leisure, and since he was the only person who could force a passage through the wood nobody had been able to pursue him.

While the prince was wondering what to believe, an old peasant took up the tale.

"Your highness," said he, "more than 50 years ago I heard my father say that in this castle lies a princess, the most beautiful that has ever been seen. It is her doom to sleep there for a hundred years, and then to be awakened by a king's son, for whose coming she waits."

This story fired the young prince. He jumped immediately to the conclusion that it was for him to see so gay an adventure through, and impelled alike by the wish for love and glory, he resolved to set about it on the spot.

Hardly had he taken a step towards the woods when the tall trees, the brambles and the thorns, separated of themselves and made a path for him. He turned in the direction of the castle, and espied it at the end of a long avenue. This avenue he entered, and was surprised to notice that the trees closed up again as soon as he had passed, so that none of his retinue were able to follow him. A young and gallant prince is always brave, however; so he continued on his way, and presently reached a large fore-court.

The sight that now met his gaze was enough to fill him with an icy fear. The silence of the place was dreadful, and death seemed all about him. The recumbent figures of men and animals had all the appearance of being lifeless, until he perceived by the pimply noses and ruddy faces of the porters that they merely slept. It was plain, too, from their glasses, in which were still some dregs of wine, that they had fallen asleep while drinking.

The prince made his way into a great courtyard, paved with marble, and mounting the staircase entered the guardroom. Here the guards were lined up on either side in two ranks, their muskets on their shoulders, snoring their hardest. Through several apartments crowded with ladies and gentlemen in waiting, some seated, some standing, but all asleep, he pushed on, and so came at last to a chamber which was decked all over with gold. There he encountered the most beautiful sight he had ever seen. Reclining upon a bed, the curtains of which on every side were drawn back, was a princess of seemingly some 15 or 16 summers, whose radiant beauty had an almost unearthly luster.

Trembling in his admiration he drew near and went on his knees beside her. At the same moment, the hour of disenchantment having come, the princess awoke, and bestowed upon him a look more tender than a first glance might seem to warrant.

"Is it you, dear prince?" she said; "You have been long in coming!"

Charmed by these words, and especially by the manner in which they were said, the prince scarcely knew how to express his delight and gratification. He declared that he loved her better than he loved himself. His words were faltering, but they pleased her the more for that. The less there is of eloquence, the more there is of love.

Her embarrassment was less than his, and that is not to be wondered at, since she had had time to think of what she would say to him. It seems (although the story says nothing about it) that the good fairy had beguiled her long slumber with pleasant dreams. To be brief, after four hours of talking they had not succeeded in uttering one half of the things they had to say to each other.

Jack lives with his mother, and they are very poor. Until one day Jack goes out to sell their cow and comes back with five magical beans. The beans are the key to their fortune.

Jack and the Beanstalk

JOSEPH JACOBS

There was once upon a time a poor widow who had an only son named Jack, and a cow named Milky-white. And all they had to live on was the milk the cow gave every morning, which they carried to the market and sold. But one morning Milky-white gave no milk, and they didn't know what to do.

"What shall we do, what shall we do?" said the widow, wringing her hands.

"Cheer up, mother, I'll go and work somewhere," said Jack.

"We've tried that before, and nobody would take you," said his mother; "we must sell Milky-white and with the money start a shop, or something."

"All right, mother," says Jack; "it's market-day today, and I'll soon sell Milky-white, and then we'll see what we can do."

So he took the cow's halter in his hand, and off he started. He hadn't gone far when he met a funny-looking old man, who said to him: "Good morning, Jack."

"Good morning to you," said Jack, and wondered how he knew his name.

"Well, Jack, and where are you off to?" said the man.

"I'm going to market to sell our cow there."

"Oh, you look the proper sort of chap to sell cows," said the man; "I wonder if you know how many beans make five."

"Two in each hand and one in your mouth," says Jack, as sharp as a needle.

"Right you are," says the man, "and here they are, the very beans themselves," he went on, pulling out of his pocket a number of strange-looking beans. "As you are so sharp," says he, "I don't mind doing a swap with you—your cow for these beans."

"Go along," says Jack; "wouldn't you like it?"

"Ah! you don't know what these beans are," said the man, "If you plant them overnight, by morning they grow right up to the sky."

"Really?" said Jack; "you don't say so."

"Yes, that is so, and if it doesn't turn out to be true you can have your cow back."

"Right," says Jack, and hands him over Milky-white's halter and pockets the beans.

Back goes Jack home, and as he hadn't gone very far it wasn't dusk by the time he got to his door.

"Back already, Jack?" said his mother; "I see you haven't got Milky-white, so you've sold her. How much did you get for her?"

"You'll never guess, mother," says Jack.

"No, you don't say so. Good boy! Five pounds, ten, fifteen, no, it can't be twenty."

"I told you you couldn't guess. What do you say to these beans; they're magical, plant them overnight and—"

"What!" says Jack's mother, "have you been such a fool, such a dolt, such an idiot, as to give away Milky-white, the best milker in the parish, and prime beef to boot, for a set of paltry beans? Take that! Take that! Take that! And as for your precious beans, here they go out of the window. And now off with you to bed. Not a sup shall you drink, and not a bit shall you swallow this very night."

So Jack went upstairs to his little room in the attic, and sad and sorry he was, to be sure, as much for his mother's sake, as for the loss of his supper.

At last he dropped off to sleep.

When he woke up, the room looked so funny. The sun was shining into part of it, and yet all the rest was quite dark and shady. So Jack jumped up and dressed himself and went to the window. And what do you think he saw? Why, the beans his mother had thrown out of the window into the garden had sprung up into a big beanstalk which went up and up and up till it reached the sky. So the man spoke truth after all.

The beanstalk grew up quite close past Jack's window, so all he had to do was to open it and give a jump on to the beanstalk which ran up just like a big ladder. So Jack climbed, and he climbed and he climbed and he climbed and he climbed and he climbed and he climbed till at last he reached the sky. And when he got there he found a long broad road going as straight as a dart. So he walked along and he walked along and he walked along till he came to a great big tall house, and on the doorstep there was a great big tall woman.

"Good morning, mom," says Jack, quite polite-like. "Could you be so kind as to give me some breakfast?" For he hadn't had anything to eat, you know, the night before and was as hungry as a hunter.

"It's breakfast you want, is it?" says the great big tall woman, "it's breakfast you'll be if you don't move off from here. My man is an ogre and there's nothing he likes better than boys broiled on toast. You'd better be moving on or he'll be coming.

"Goodness gracious me! It's my old man," said the ogre's wife, "what on earth shall I do? Come along quick and jump in here." And she bundled Jack into the oven just as the ogre came in.

He was a big one, to be sure. At his belt he had three calves strung up by the heels, and he unhooked them and threw them down on the table and said, "Here, wife, broil me a couple of these for breakfast. Ah! what's this I smell?

> *"Fee-fi-fo-fum,*
> *I smell the blood of an Englishman,*
> *Be he alive, or be he dead,*
> *I'll have his bones to grind my bread."*

"Nonsense, dear," said his wife, "you're dreaming. Or perhaps you smell the scraps of that little boy you liked so much for yesterday's dinner. Here, you go and have a wash and tidy up and by the time you come back your breakfast'll be ready for you."

So off the ogre went, and Jack was just going to jump out of the oven and run away when the woman told him not. "Wait till he's asleep," says she; "he always has a doze after breakfast."

Well, the ogre had his breakfast, and after that he goes to a big chest and takes out a

couple of bags of gold, and down he sits and counts till at last his head began to nod and he began to snore till the whole house shook again.

Then Jack crept out on tiptoe from his oven, and as he was passing the ogre he took one of the bags of gold under his arm, and off he pelters till he came to the beanstalk, and then he threw down the bag of gold, which, of course, fell into his mother's garden, and then he climbed down and climbed down till at last he got home and told his mother and showed her the gold and said: "Well mother, wasn't I right about the beans? They are really magical, you see."

So they lived on the bag of gold for some time, but at last they came to the end of it, and Jack made up his mind to try his luck once more at the top of the beanstalk. So one fine morning he rose up early, and got on to the beanstalk and he climbed and he climbed and he climbed and he climbed and he climbed and he climbed till at last he came out on to the road again and up to the great tall house he had been to before. There, sure enough, was the great tall woman a-standing on the doorstep.

"Good morning, mom," says Jack, as bold as brass, "could you be so good as to give me something to eat?"

"Go away, my boy," said the big tall woman, "or else my man will eat you up for breakfast. But aren't you the youngster who came here once before? Do you know, that every day my man missed one of his bags of gold."

"That's strange, mum," said Jack, "I dare say I could tell you something about that, but I'm so hungry I can't speak till I've had something to eat."

Well, the big tall woman was so curious that she took him in and gave him something to eat. But he had scarcely begun munching it as slowly as he could when thump! thump! they heard the giant's footstep, and his wife hid Jack away in the oven.

All happened as it did before. In came the ogre as he did before, said, "Fee-fi-fo-fum," and has his breakfast of three broiled oxen. Then he said, "Wife, bring me the hen that lays the golden eggs." So she brought it, and the ogre said, "Lay," and it laid an egg all of gold. And then the ogre began to nod his head, and to snore till the house shook.

Then Jack crept out of the oven on tiptoe and caught hold of the golden hen, and was off before you could say "Jack Robinson." But this time the hen gave a cackle which woke the ogre, and just as Jack got out of the house he heard him calling, "Wife, wife, what have you done with my golden hen?"

And the wife said, "Why, my dear?"

But that was all Jack heard, for he rushed off to the beanstalk and climbed down like a house on fire. And when he got home he showed his mother the wonderful hen, and said "Lay" to it; and it laid a golden egg every time he said "Lay."

Well, Jack was not happy, and wanted to try again. So, he rose in the morning and climbed to the top. But this time he knew better than to go straight to the ogre's house. And when he got near it, he waited behind a bush till he saw the ogre's wife come out with a pail to get some water, and then he crept into the house and got into the copper. He hadn't been there long when he heard thump! thump! thump! as before, and in came the ogre and his wife.

"Fee-fi-fo-fum, I smell the blood of an Englishman," cried out the ogre. "I smell him, wife, I smell him."

"Do you, my dearie?" says the ogre's wife. "Then, if it's that little rogue that stole your gold and the hen that laid the golden eggs he's sure to have got into the oven." And they both rushed to the oven. But Jack wasn't here, luckily, and the ogre's wife said, "There you are again with your fee-fi-fo-fum. Why, of course, it's the boy you caught last night that I've just broiled for your breakfast. How forgetful I am, and how careless you are not to know the difference between live and dead after all these years."

So the ogre sat down to the breakfast and ate it, but every now and then he would mutter, "Well, I could have sworn—" and he'd get up and search the larder and the cupboards and everything, only, luckily, he didn't think of the copper.

After breakfast was over, the ogre called out, "Wife, wife, bring me my golden harp."

So she brought it and put it on the table before him. Then he said, "Sing!" and the golden harp sang most beautifully. And it went on singing till the ogre fell asleep, and commenced to snore like thunder.

Then Jack lifted up the copper-lid very quietly and got down like a mouse and crept on hands and knees till he came to the table, when up he crawled, caught hold of the golden harp and dashed with it towards the door. But the harp called out quite loud, "Master! Master!" and the ogre woke up just in time to see Jack running off with his harp.

Jack ran as fast as he could, and the ogre came rushing after. When the ogre got to the beanstalk, he saw Jack disappear and begin climbing down. Well, the ogre didn't like trusting himself to such a ladder, and he stood and waited, so Jack got another start. But just then the harp cried out, "Master! Master" and the ogre swung himself down on to the beanstalk, which shook with his weight. Down climbs Jack, and after him climbed the ogre. By this time Jack had climbed down and climbed down and climbed down till he was very nearly home. So he called out, "Mother! Mother! Bring me an axe, bring me an axe." And his mother came rushing out with the axe in her hand, but when she came to the beanstalk she stood stock still with fright, for there she saw the ogre with his legs just through the clouds.

But Jack jumped down and got hold of the axe and gave a chop at the beanstalk which cut it half in two. The ogre felt the beanstalk shake and quiver, so he stopped to see what was the matter. Then Jack gave another chop with the axe, and the beanstalk was cut in two and began to topple over. Then the ogre fell down and broke his crown, and the beanstalk came toppling after.

Then Jack showed his mother his golden harp, and what with showing that and selling the golden eggs, Jack and his mother became very rich, and he married a great princess, and they lived happily ever after.

Dorothy awakes after a tornado to find that she and her house have landed with a bump in the curious land of the Munchkins. As kind as the Munchkins are, Dorothy wants only to return home to Kansas. She sets off on a journey and, along the way, meets the Tin Woodman, the Cowardly Lion, and the Scarecrow. Dorothy is lucky to have met these friends for the trip turns out to be full of adventures for everyone.

The Wizard of Oz

L. FRANK BAUM

CHAPTER II
THE COUNCIL WITH THE MUNCHKINS

She was awakened by a shock so sudden and severe that if Dorothy had not been lying on the soft bed she might have been hurt. As it was, the jar made her catch her breath and wonder what had happened; and Toto put his cold little nose into her face and whined dismally. Dorothy sat up and noticed that the house was not moving; nor was it dark, for the bright sunshine came in at the window, flooding the little room. She sprang from her bed and with Toto at her heels ran and opened the door.

The little girl gave a cry of amazement and looked about her, her eyes growing bigger and bigger at the wonderful sights she saw.

The cyclone had set the house down, very gently—for a cyclone—in the midst of a country of marvelous beauty. There were lovely patches of green all about, with stately trees bearing rich and luscious fruits. Banks of gorgeous flowers

were on every hand, and birds with rare and brilliant plumage sang and fluttered in the trees and bushes. A little way off was a small brook, rushing and sparkling along between green banks, and murmuring in a voice very grateful to a little girl who had lived so long on the dry, gray prairies.

While she stood looking eagerly at the strange and beautiful sights, she noticed coming toward her a group of the queerest people she had ever seen. They were not as big as the grown folk she had always been used to; but neither were they very small. In fact, they seemed about as tall as Dorothy, who was a well-grown child for her age, although they were, so far as looks go, many years older.

Three were men and one a woman, and all were oddly dressed. They wore round hats that rose to a small point a foot above their heads, with little bells around the brims that tinkled sweetly as they moved. The hats of the men were blue; the little woman's hat was white, and she wore a white gown that hung in plaits from her shoulders; over it were sprinkled little stars that glistened in the sun like diamonds. The men were dressed in blue, of the same shade as their hats, and wore well-polished boots with a deep roll of blue at the tops. The men, Dorothy thought, were about as old as Uncle Henry, for two of them had beards. But the little woman was doubtless much older: her face was covered with wrinkles, her hair was nearly white, and she walked rather stiffly.

When these people drew near the house where Dorothy was standing in the doorway, they paused and whispered among themselves, as if afraid to come farther. But the little old woman walked up to Dorothy, made a low bow and said, in a sweet voice:

"You are welcome, most noble Sorceress, to the land of the Munchkins. We are so grateful to you for having killed the wicked Witch of the East, and for setting our people free from bondage."

Dorothy listened to this speech with wonder. What could the little woman possibly mean by calling her a sorceress, and saying she had killed the wicked Witch of the East? Dorothy was an innocent, harmless little girl, who had been carried by a cyclone many miles from home; and she had never killed anything in all her life.

But the little woman evidently expected her to answer; so Dorothy said, with hesitation, "You are very kind; but there must be some mistake. I have not killed anything."

"Your house did, anyway," replied the little old woman, with a laugh; "and that is the same thing. See!" she continued, pointing to the corner of the house; "there are her two toes, still sticking out from under a block of wood."

Dorothy looked and gave a little cry of fright. There, indeed, just under the corner of the great beam the house rested on, two feet were sticking out, shod in silver shoes with pointed toes.

"Oh, dear! oh, dear!" cried Dorothy, clasping her hands together in dismay; "the house must have fallen on her. What ever shall we do?"

"There is nothing to be done," said the little woman calmly.

"But who was she?" asked Dorothy.

"She was the wicked Witch of the East, as I said," answered the little woman. "She has held all the Munchkins in bondage for many years, making them slave for her night and day. Now they are all set free, and are grateful to you for the favor."

"Who are the Munchkins?" enquired Dorothy.

"They are the people who live in this land of the East, where the wicked Witch ruled."

"Are you a Munchkin?" asked Dorothy.

"No, but I am their friend, although I live in the land of the North. When they saw the Witch of the East was dead, the Munchkins sent a swift messenger to me, and I came at once. I am the Witch of the North."

"Oh, gracious!" cried Dorothy; "are you a real witch?"

"Yes, indeed"; answered the little woman. "But I am a good witch, and the people love me. I am not as powerful as the wicked Witch was who ruled here, or I should have set the people free myself."

"But I thought all witches were wicked," said the girl, who was half frightened at facing a real witch.

"Oh, no; that is a great mistake. There were only four witches in all the Land of Oz, and two of them, those who live in the North and the South, are good witches. I know this is true, for I am one of them myself, and cannot be mistaken. Those who dwelt in the East and the West were, indeed, wicked witches; but now that you have killed one of them, there is but one wicked Witch in all the Land of Oz—the one who lives in the West."

"But," said Dorothy, after a moment's thought, "Aunt Em has told me that the witches were all dead—years and years ago."

"Who is Aunt Em?" inquired the old woman.

"She is my aunt who lives in Kansas, where I came from."

The Witch of the North seemed to think for a time, with her head bowed and her eyes upon the ground. Then she looked up and said, "I do not know where Kansas is, for I have never heard that country mentioned before. But tell me, is it a civilized country?"

"Oh, yes," replied Dorothy.

"Then that accounts for it. In the civilized countries I believe there are no witches left; nor wizards, nor sorceresses, nor magicians. But, you see, the Land of Oz has never been civilized, for we are cut off from all the rest of the world. Therefore we still have witches and wizards amongst us."

"Who are the wizards?" asked Dorothy.

"Oz himself is the Great Wizard," answered the Witch, sinking her voice to a whisper. "He is more powerful than all the rest of us together. He lives in the City of Emeralds."

Dorothy was going to ask another question, but just then the Munchkins, who had been standing silently by, gave a loud shout and pointed to the corner of the house where the Wicked witch had been lying.

"What is it?" asked the little old woman; and looked, and began to laugh. The feet of the dead Witch had disappeared entirely and nothing was left but the silver shoes.

"She was so old," explained the Witch of the North, "that she dried up quickly in the sun. That is the end of her. But the silver shoes are yours, and you shall have them to wear." She reached down and picked up the shoes, and after shaking the dust out of them handed them to Dorothy.

"The Witch of the East was proud of those silver shoes," said one of the Munchkins; "and there is some charm connected with them; but what it is we never know."

Dorothy carried the shoes into the house and placed them on the table. Then she came out again to the Munchkins and said, "I am anx-

ious to get back to my aunt and uncle, for I am sure they will worry about me. Can you help me find my way?"

The Munchkins and the Witch first looked at one another, and then at Dorothy, and then shook their heads.

"At the East, not far from here," said one, "there is a great desert, and none could live to cross it."

"It is the same at the South," said another, "for I have been there and seen it. The South is the country of the Quadlings."

"I am told," said the third man, "that it is the same at the West. And that country, where the Winkies live, is ruled by the wicked Witch of the West, who would make you her slave if you passed her way."

"The North is my home," said the old lady, "and at its edge is the same great desert that surrounds this land of Oz. I'm afraid, my dear, you will have to live with us."

Dorothy began to sob at this, for she felt lonely among all these strange people. Her tears seemed to grieve the kind-hearted Munchkins, for they immediately took out their hand-kerchiefs and began to weep also. As for the little old woman, she took off her cap and balanced the point on the end of her nose, while she counted "one, two, three," in a solemn voice. At once the cap changed to a slate, on which was written in big, white chalk marks: LET DOROTHY GO TO THE CITY OF EMERALDS.

The little old woman took the slate from her nose, and, having read the words on it, asked, "Is your name Dorothy, my dear?"

"Yes," answered the child, looking up and drying her tears.

"Then you must go to the City of Emeralds. Perhaps Oz will help you."

"Where is this City?" asked Dorothy.

"It is exactly in the center of the country, and is ruled by Oz, the Great Wizard I told you of."

"Is he a good man?" inquired the girl, anxiously.

"He is a good Wizard. Whether he is a man or not I cannot tell, for I have never seen him."

"How can I get there?" asked Dorothy.

"You must walk. It is a long journey, through a country that is sometimes pleasant and sometimes dark and terrible. However, I will use all the magic arts I know of to keep you from harm."

"Won't you go with me?" pleaded the girl, who had begun to look upon the little old woman as her only friend.

"No, I cannot do that," she replied; "but I will give you my kiss, and no one will dare injure a person who has been kissed by the Witch of the North."

She came close to Dorothy and kissed her gently on the forehead. Where her lips touched the girl they left a round, shining mark, as Dorothy found out soon after.

"The road to the City of Emeralds is paved with yellow brick," said the Witch; "so you cannot miss it. When you get to Oz do not be afraid of him, but tell your story and ask him to help you. Good-bye, my dear."

The three Munchkins bowed low to her and wished her a pleasant journey, after which they walked away through the trees. The Witch gave Dorothy a friendly little nod, whirled around on her left heel three times, and straightaway disappeared, much to the surprise of little Toto, who barked loudly when she had gone, because he had been afraid even to growl while she stood by.

But Dorothy, knowing her to be a witch, had expected her to disappear in just that way, and was not surprised in the least.

CHAPTER VII
THE DEADLY POPPY FIELD

Our little party of travelers awakened next morning refreshed and full of hope, and Dorothy breakfasted like a princess off peaches and plums from the trees beside the river.

Behind them was the dark forest they had passed safely through, although they had suffered many discouragements; but before them was a lovely, sunny country that seemed to beckon them to the Emerald City.

To be sure, the broad river now cut them off from this beautiful land; but the raft was nearly done, and after the Tin Woodman had cut a few more logs and fastened them together with wooden pins, they were ready to start. Dorothy sat down in the middle of the raft and held Toto in her arms. When the Cowardly Lion stepped upon the raft it tipped badly, for he was big and heavy; but the Scarecrow and the Tin Woodman stood upon the other end to steady it, and they had long poles in their hands to push the raft through the water.

They got along quite well at first, but when they reached the middle of the river the swift current swept the raft down stream, farther and farther away from the road of yellow brick; and the water grew so deep that the long poles would not touch the bottom.

"This is bad," said the Tin Woodman, "for if we cannot get to the land we shall be carried into the country of the wicked Witch of the West, and she will enchant us and make us her slaves."

"And then I should get no brains," said the Scarecrow.

"And I should get no courage," said the Cowardly Lion.

"And I should get no heart," said the Tin Woodman.

"And I should never get back to Kansas," said Dorothy.

"We must certainly get to the Emerald City if we can," the Scarecrow continued, and he pushed so hard on his long pole that it stuck fast in the mud at the bottom of the river, and before he could pull it out again, or let go, the raft was swept away and the poor Scarecrow was left clinging to the pole in the middle of the river.

"Good bye!" he called after them, and they were very sorry to leave him; indeed, the Tin Woodman began to cry, but fortunately remembered that he might rust, and so dried his tears on Dorothy's apron.

Of course this was a bad thing for the Scarecrow.

"I am worse off than when I first met Dorothy," he thought. "Then, I was stuck on a pole in a cornfield, where I could make believe scare the crows, at any rate; but surely there is no use for a Scarecrow stuck on a pole in the middle of a river. I am afraid I shall never have any brains, after all!"

Down the stream the raft floated, and the poor Scarecrow was left far behind. Then the Lion said: "Something must be done to save us. I think I can swim to the shore and pull the raft after me, if you will only hold fast to the tip of my tail."

So he sprang into the water and the Tin Woodman caught fast hold of his tail, then the Lion began to swim with all his might toward the shore.

It was hard work, although he was so big; but by and by they were drawn out of the current, and then Dorothy took the Tin Woodman's long pole and helped push the raft to the land.

They were all tired out when they reached the shore at last and stepped off upon the pretty green grass, and they also knew that the stream had carried them a long ways past the road of yellow brick that led to the Emerald City.

"What shall we do now?" asked the Tin Woodman, as the Lion lay down on the grass to let the sun dry him.

"We must get back to the road, in some way," said Dorothy.

"The best plan will be to walk along the river bank until we come to the road again," remarked the Lion.

So, when they were rested, Dorothy picked up her basket and they started along the grassy bank, back to the road from which the river had carried them. It was a lovely country, with plenty of flowers and fruit trees and sunshine to cheer them, and had they not felt so sorry for the poor Scarecrow they could have been very happy.

They walked along as fast as they could, Dorothy only stopping once to pick a beautiful flower; and after a time the Tin Woodman cried out:

"Look!"

Then they all looked at the river and saw the Scarecrow perched upon his pole in the middle of the water, looking lonely and sad.

"What can we do to save him?" asked Dorothy.

The Lion and the Woodman both shook their heads, for they did not know. So they sat down upon the bank and gazed wistfully at the Scarecrow until a Stork flew by, which, seeing them, stopped to rest at the water's edge.

"Who are you, and where are you going?" asked the Stork.

"I am Dorothy," answered the girl; "and these are my friends, the Tin Woodman and the Cowardly Lion; and we are going to the Emerald City."

"This isn't the road," said the Stork, as she twisted her long neck and looked sharply at the queer party.

"I know it," returned Dorothy, "but we have lost the Scarecrow, and are wondering how we shall get him again."

"Where is he?" asked the Stork.

"Over there in the river," answered the girl.

"If he wasn't so big and heavy I would get him for you," remarked the Stork.

"He isn't heavy a bit," said Dorothy, eagerly, "for he is stuffed with straw; and if you will bring him back to us we shall thank you ever and ever so much."

"Well, I'll try," said the Stork, "but if I find he is too heavy to carry I shall have to drop him in the river again."

So the big bird flew into the air and over the water till she came to where the Scarecrow was perched upon his pole. Then the Stork with her great claws grabbed the Scarecrow by the arm and carried him up into the air and back to the bank, where Dorothy and the Lion and the Tin Woodman and Toto were sitting.

When the Scarecrow found himself among his friends again he was so happy that he hugged them all, even the Lion and Toto; and as they walked along he sang "To-de-ri-de-oh!" at every step, he felt so gay.

Alice is having an average, dull day sitting with her sister outside on a river bank. That is, until she sees a white rabbit hustling by her—taking a watch out of its waistcoat pocket! Thinking this a very curious sight, she follows the rabbit down the rabbit-hole, plummeting past cupboards and bookshelves. Thus begins a day full of adventures in which Alice encounters some very odd creatures. Here she comes across the house of the March Hare. It has chimneys shaped like ears, and a roof thatched with fur.

Alice in Wonderland

LEWIS CARROLL

CHAPTER VII
A MAD TEA-PARTY

There was a table set out under a tree in front of the house, and the March Hare and the Hatter were having tea at it: a Dormouse was sitting between them, fast asleep, and the other two were using it as a cushion, resting their elbows on it, and talking over its head. "Very uncomfortable for the Dormouse," thought Alice; "only as it's asleep, I suppose it doesn't mind."

The table was a large one, but the three were all crowded together at one corner of it. "No room! No room!" they cried out when they saw Alice coming.

"There's plenty of room!" said Alice indignantly, and she sat down in a large armchair at one end of the table.

"Have some wine," the March Hare said in an encouraging tone.

Alice looked all around the table, but there was nothing on it but tea. "I don't see any wine," she remarked.

"There isn't any," said the March Hare.

"Then it wasn't very civil of you to offer it," said Alice angrily.

"It wasn't very civil of you to sit down without being invited," said the March Hare.

"I didn't know it was your table," said Alice, "It's laid for a great many more than three."

"Your hair wants cutting," said the Hatter. He had been looking at Alice for some time with great curiosity, and this was his first speech.

"You should learn not to make personal remarks," Alice said with some severity, "it's very rude."

The Hatter opened his eyes very wide on hearing this; but all he said was, "Why is a raven like a writing-desk?"

"Come, we shall have some fun now!" thought Alice. "I'm glad they've begun asking riddles—I believe I can guess that," she added aloud.

"Do you mean that you think you can find out the answer to it?" said the March Hare.

"Exactly so," said Alice.

"Then you should say what you mean," the March Hare went on.

"I do," Alice hastily replied; "at least—at least I mean what I say—that's the same thing, you know."

"Not the same thing a bit!" said the Hatter. "Why, you might just as well say that 'I see what I eat' is the same thing as 'I eat what I see'!"

"You might just as well say," added the March Hare, "that 'I like what I get' is the same thing as 'I get what I like'!"

"You might just as well say," added the Dormouse, which seemed to be talking in its sleep, "that 'I breathe when I sleep' is the same things as 'I sleep when I breathe'!"

"It is the same thing with you," said the Hatter, and here the conversation dropped, and the party sat silent for a minute, while Alice thought over all she could remember about ravens and writing-desks, which wasn't much.

The Hatter was the first to break the silence. "What day of the month is it?" he said, turning to Alice, he had taken his watch out of his pocket, and was looking at it uneasily, shaking it every now and then, and holding it to his ear.

Alice considered a little, and then said, "The fourth."

"Two days wrong!" sighed the Hatter. "I told you butter wouldn't suit the works!" he added, looking angrily at the March Hare.

"It was the best butter," the March Hare meekly replied.

"Yes, but some crumbs must have got in as well," the Hatter grumbled; "you shouldn't have put it in with the bread-knife."

The March Hare took the watch and looked at it gloomily; then he dipped it into his cup of tea, and looked at it again; but he could think of nothing better to say than his first remark, "It was the best butter, you know."

Alice had been looking over his shoulder with some curiosity. "What a funny watch!" she remarked. "It tells the day of the month, and doesn't tell what o'clock it is!"

"Why should it?" muttered the Hatter. "Does your watch tell you what year it is?"

"Of course not," Alice replied very readily; "but that's because it stays the same year for such a long time together."

"Which is just the case with mine," said the Hatter.

Alice felt dreadfully puzzled. The Hatter's remark seemed to her to have no sort of meaning in it, and yet it was certainly English. "I don't quite understand you," she said, as politely as she could.

"The Dormouse is asleep again," said the Hatter, and he poured a little hot tea upon its nose.

The Dormouse shook its head impatiently, and said, without opening its eyes, "Of course, of course; just what I was going to remark myself."

"Have you guessed the riddle yet?" the Hatter said, turning to Alice again.

"No, I give it up," Alice replied. "What's the answer?"

"I haven't the slightest idea," said the Hatter.

"Nor I," said the March Hare.

Alice sighed wearily. "I think you might do something better with the time," she said, "than wasting it in asking riddles that have no answers."

"If you knew Time as well as I do," said the Hatter, "you wouldn't talk about wasting it. It's him."

"I don't know what you mean," said Alice.

"Of course you don't!" the Hatter said, tossing his head contemptuously. "I dare say you never even spoke to Time!"

"Perhaps not," Alice cautiously replied; "but I know I have to beat time when I learn music."

"Ah! That accounts for it," said the Hatter. "He won't stand beating. Now, if you only kept on good terms with him, he'd do almost anything you liked with the clock. For instance, suppose it were nine o'clock in the morning, just time to begin lessons; you'd only have to whisper a hint to Time, and round goes the clock in a twinkling! Half-past one, time for dinner!"

("I only wish it was," the March Hare said to itself in a whisper.)

"That would be grand, certainly," said Alice thoughtfully; "but then—I shouldn't be hungry for it, you know."

"Not at first, perhaps," said the Hatter; "but you could keep it to half-past one as long as you liked."

"Is that the way you manage?" Alice asked.

The Hatter shook his head mournfully. "Not I!" he replied. "We quarreled last March—just before he went mad, you know"—pointing with his teaspoon

at the March Hare,—"it was at the great concert given by the Queen of Hearts, and I had to sing

Twinkle, twinkle, little bat!
How I wonder what you're at!

You know the song, perhaps?"

"I've heard something like it," said Alice.

"It goes on, you know," the Hatter continued, "in this way—

Up above the world you fly,
Like a tea-tray in the sky.
Twinkle, twinkle—"

Here the Dormouse shook itself, and began singing in its sleep "Twinkle, twinkle, twinkly, twinkle—" and went on so long that they had to pinch it to make it stop.

"Well, I'd hardly finished the first verse," said the Hatter, "when the Queen bawled out 'He's murdering the time! Off with his head!'"

"How dreadfully savage!" exclaimed Alice.

"And ever since that," the Hatter went on in a mournful tone, "he won't do a thing I ask! It's always six o'clock now."

A bright idea came into Alice's head. "Is that the reason so many tea-things are put out here?" she asked.

"Yes, that's it," said the Hatter with a sigh; "it's always tea-time, and we've no time to wash the things between whiles."

"Then you keep moving around, I suppose?" said Alice.

"Exactly so," said the Hatter, "as the things get used up."

"But what happens when you come to the beginning again?" Alice ventured to ask.

"Suppose we change the subject," the March Hare interrupted, yawning. "I'm getting tired of this. I vote the young lady tells us a story."

"I'm afraid I don't know one," said Alice, rather alarmed at the proposal.

"Then the Dormouse shall!" they both cried. "Wake up, Dormouse!" And they pinched it on both sides at once.

The Dormouse slowly opened its eyes. "I wasn't asleep," it said in a hoarse, feeble voice, "I heard every word you fellows were saying."

"Tell us a story!" said the March Hare.

"Yes, please do!" pleaded Alice.

"And be quick about it," added the Hatter, "or you'll be asleep again before it's done."

"Once upon a time there were three little sisters," the Dormouse began in a great hurry; "and their names were Elsie, Lacie, and Tillie; and they lived at the bottom of a well—"

"What did they live on?" said Alice, who always took a great interest in questions of eating and drinking.

"They lived on a treacle," said the Dormouse, after thinking a minute or two.

"They couldn't have done that, you know," Alice gently remarked. "They'd have been ill."

"So, they were," said the Dormouse, "very ill."

Alice tried a little to fancy herself what such an extraordinary way of living would be like, but it puzzled her too much, so she went on: "But why did they live at the bottom of a well?"

"Take some more tea," the March Hare said to Alice, very earnestly.

"I've had nothing yet," Alice replied in an offended tone, "so I can't take more."

"You mean you can't take less," said the Hatter, "it's very easy to take more than nothing."

"Nobody asked your opinion," said Alice.

"Who's making personal remarks now?" the Hatter asked triumphantly.

Alice did not quite know what to say to this, so she helped herself to some tea and bread-and-butter, and then turned to the Dormouse, and repeated her question. "Why did they live at the bottom of a well?"

The Dormouse again took a minute or two to think about it, and then said, "It was a treacle-well."

"There's no such thing!" Alice was beginning very angrily, but the Hatter and the March Hare went "Sh! Sh!" and the Dormouse sulkily remarked, "If you can't be civil, you'd better finish the story for yourself."

"No, please go on!" Alice said very humbly. "I won't interrupt you again. I dare say there may be one."

"One indeed!" said the Dormouse indignantly. However, he consented to go on. "And so these three little sisters—they were learning to draw, you know—"

"What did they draw?" said Alice, quite forgetting her promise.

"Treacle," said the Dormouse, without considering at all, this time.

"I want a clean cup," interrupted the Hatter; "let's all move one place on."

He moved on as he spoke, and the Dormouse followed him: the March Hare moved into the Dormouse's place, and Alice rather unwillingly took the place of the March Hare. The Hatter was the only one who got any advantage from the change; and Alice was a good deal worse off than before, as the March Hare had just upset the milk-jug into his plate.

Alice did not wish to offend the Dormouse again, so she began very cautiously: "But I don't understand. Where did they draw the treacle from?"

"You can draw water out of a water-well," said the Hatter; "so I should think you could draw treacle out of a treacle-well—eh, stupid?"

"But they were in the well," Alice said to the Dormouse, not choosing to notice this last remark.

"Of course they were," said the Dormouse; "well in."

This answer so confused poor Alice, that she let the Dormouse go on for some time without interrupting it.

"They were learning to draw," the Dormouse went on, yawning and rubbing its eyes, for it was getting very sleepy; "and they drew all manner of things—everything that begins with an M—"

"Why with an M?" said Alice.

"Why not?" said the March Hare.

Alice was silent.

The Dormouse had closed its eyes by this time, and was going off into a doze; but, on being pinched by the Hatter, it woke up again with a little shriek, and went on: "—that begins with an M, such as mouse-traps, and the moon, and memory, and muchness—you know you say things are 'much of a muchness'—did you ever see such a thing as a drawing of a muchness!"

"Really, now you ask me," said Alice, very much confused, "I don't think—"

"Then you shouldn't talk," said the Hatter. This piece of rudeness was more than Alice could bear: she got up in great disgust, and walked off; the Dormouse fell asleep instantly, and neither of the others took the least notice of her going, though she looked back once or twice, half hoping that they would call after her. The last time she saw them, they were trying to put the Dormouse into the teapot.

"At any rate I'll never go there again!" said Alice, as she picked her way through the wood. "It's the stupidest tea-party I ever was at in all my life!"

Just as she said this, she noticed that one of the trees had a door leading right into it. "That's very curious!" she thought. "But everything's curious today. I think I may as well go in at once." And in she went.

Once more she found herself in the long hall, and close to the little glass table. "Now, I'll manage better this time," she said to herself, and began by taking the little golden key, and unlocking the door that led into the garden. Then she set to work nibbling at the mushroom (she had kept a piece of it in her pocket) till she was about a foot high: then she walked down the little passage, and then—she found herself at last in the beautiful garden, among the bright flower-beds and the cool fountains.

There are four sisters in the March family; Jo, Meg, Beth, and Amy. They are very close and share many happy and sad times together. When Jo's short story wins first place in a contest and is published, the whole family is ecstatic.

Little Women

LOUISA MAY ALCOTT

CHAPTER 27
LITERARY LESSONS

Fortune suddenly smiled upon Jo, and dropped a good-luck penny in her path. Not a golden penny, exactly, but I doubt if half a million would have given more real happiness than did the little sum that came to her in this wise.

Every few weeks she would shut herself up in her room, put on her scribbling suit, and "fall into a vortex," as she expressed it, writing away at her novel with all her heart and soul, for till that was finished she could find no peace. Her "scribbling suit" consisted of a black woolen pinafore on which she could wipe her pen at will, and a cap of the same material, adorned with a cheerful red bow, into which she bundled her hair when the decks were cleared for action. This cap was a beacon to the inquiring eyes of her family, who during these periods kept their distance, merely popping in their heads semi-occasionally, to ask, with interest, "Does genius burn, Jo?" They did not always venture even to ask this question, but took an observation of the cap, and judged accordingly. If this expressive article of dress was drawn low upon

the forehead, it was a sign that hard work was going on; in exciting moments it was pushed rakishly askew; and when despair seized the author it was plucked wholly off, and cast upon the floor. At such times the intruder silently withdrew; and not until the red bow was seen gayly erect upon the gifted brow, did any one dare address Jo.

She did not think herself a genius by any means; but when the writing fit came on, she gave herself up to it with entire abandon, and led a blissful life, unconscious of want, care, or bad weather, while she sat safe and happy in an imaginary world, full of friends almost as real and dear to her as any in the flesh. Sleep forsook her eyes, meals stood untasted, day and night were all too short to enjoy the happiness which blessed her only at such times, and made these hours worth living, even if they bore no other fruit. The divine afflatus usually lasted a week or two, and then she emerged from her "vortex," hungry, sleepy, cross, or despondent.

She was just recovering from one of these attacks when she was prevailed upon to escort Miss Crocker to a lecture, and in return for her virtue was rewarded with a new idea. It was a People's Course, the lecture on the Pyramids, and Jo rather wondered at the choice of such a subject for such an audience, but took it for granted that some great social evil would be remedied or some great want supplied by unfolding the glories of the Pharaohs to an audience whose thoughts were busy with the price of coal and flour, and whose lives were spent in trying to solve harder riddles than that of the Sphinx.

They were early; and while Miss Crocker set the heel of her stocking, Jo amused herself by examining the faces of the people who occupied the seat with them. On her left were two matrons, with massive foreheads, and bonnets to match, discussing Woman's Rights and making tatting. Beyond sat a pair of humble lovers, artlessly holding each other by the hand, a sombre spinster eating peppermints out of a paper bag, and an old gentleman taking his preparatory nap behind a yellow bandanna. On her right, her only neighbor was a studious-looking lad absorbed in a newspaper.

It was a pictorial sheet, and Jo examined the work of art nearest her, idly wondering what unfortuitous concatenation of circumstances needed the melodramatic illustration of an Indian in full war costume, tumbling over a precipice with a wolf at his throat, while two infuriated young gentlemen, with unnaturally small feet and big eyes, were stabbing each other close by, and a dishevelled female was flying away in the background with her mouth wide open. Pausing to turn a page, the lad saw her looking, and, with boyish good-nature, offered half his paper, saying bluntly, "Want to read it? That's a first-rate story."

Jo accepted it with a smile, for she had never outgrown her liking for lads, and soon found herself involved in the usual labyrinth of love, mystery, and murder, for the story belonged to that class of light literature in which the passions have a holiday, and when the author's invention fails, a grand catastrophe clears the stage of one half the dramatis personae, leaving the other half to exult over their downfall.

"Prime, isn't it?" asked the boy, as her eye went down the last paragraph of her portion.

"I think you and I could do as well as that if we tried," returned Jo, amused at this admiration of the trash.

"I should think I was a pretty lucky chap if I could. She makes a good living out of such stories, they say"; and he pointed to the name of Mrs. S.L.A.N.G. Northbury, under the title of the tale.

"Do you know her?" asked Jo, with sudden interest.

"No; but I read all her pieces, and I know a fellow who works in the office where this paper is printed."

"Do you say she makes a good living out of stories like this?" and Jo looked more respectfully at the agitated group of thickly sprinkled exclamation points that adorned the page.

"Guess she does! She knows just what folks like, and gets paid well for writing it."

Here the lecture began, but Jo heard very little of it, for while Professor Sands was prosing away about Belzoni, Cheops, Scarabei, and hieroglyphics, she was covertly taking down the address of the paper, and boldly resolving to try for the hundred-dollar prize offered in its columns for a sensational story. By the time the lecture ended and the audience awoke, she had built up a splendid fortune for herself (not the first founded upon paper), and was already deep in the concoction of her story, being unable to decide whether the duel should come before the elopement or after the murder.

She said nothing of her plan at home, but fell to work next day, much to the disquiet of her mother, who always looked a little anxious when "genius took to burning." Jo had never tried this style before, contenting herself with very mild romances for the "Spread Eagle." Her theatrical experience and miscellaneous reading were of service now, for they gave her some idea of dramatic effect, and supplied plot, language, and costumes. Her story was as full of desperation and despair as her limited acquaintance with those uncomfortable emotions enabled her to make it, and, having located it in Lisbon, she wound up with an earthquake, as a striking and appropriate dénouement. The manuscript was privately dispatched, accompanied by a note, modestly saying that if the tale didn't get the prize, which writer hardly dared expect, she would be very glad to receive any sum it might be considered worth.

Six weeks is a long time to wait, and a still longer time for a girl to keep a secret; but Jo did both, and was just beginning to give up all hope of ever seeing her manuscript again, when a letter arrived which almost took her breath away; for on opening it, a check for a hundred dollars fell into her lap. For a minute she stared at it as if it had been a snake, then she read her letter and began to cry. If the amiable gentleman who wrote that kindly note could have known what intense happiness he was giving a fellow-creature, I think he would devote his leisure hours, if he has any to that amusement; for Jo valued the letter more than the money, because it was encouraging; and after years of effort it was so pleasant to find that she had learned to do something, though it was only to write a sensation story.

A prouder young woman was seldom seen than she, when, having composed herself, she electrified the family by appearing before them with the letter in one hand, the check in the other, announcing that she had won the prize. Of course there was a great jubilee, and when the story came every one read and praised it; though after her father had told her that the language was good, the romance fresh and hearty, and the tragedy quite thrilling, he shook his head, and said in his unworldly way—

"You can do better than this, Jo. Aim at the highest, and never mind the money."

"I think the money is the best part of it. What will you do with such a fortune?" asked Amy, regarding the magic slip of paper with a reverential eye.

"Send Beth and mother to the seaside for a month or two," answered Jo promptly.

"Oh, how splendid! No, I can't do it, dear, it would be so selfish," cried Beth, who had clapped her thin hands, and taken a long breath, as if pining for fresh ocean-breezes; then stopped herself, and motioned away the check which her sister waved before her.

"Ah, but you shall go, I've set my heart on it; that's what I tried for, and that's why I succeeded. I never get on when I think of myself alone, so it will help me to work for you, don't you see? Besides, Marmee needs the change, and she won't leave you, so you must go. Won't it be fun to see you come home plump and rosy again? Hurray for Dr. Jo, who always cures her patients!"

To the seaside they went, after much discussion; and though Beth didn't come home as plump and rosy as could be desired, she was much better, while Mrs. March declared she felt ten years younger; so Jo was satisfied with the investment of her prize money and fell to work with a cheery spirit, bent on earning more of those delightful checks. She did earn several that year, and began to feel herself a power in the house; for by the magic of a pen, her "rubbish" turned into comforts for them all. "The Duke's Daughter" paid the butcher's bill, "A Phantom Hand" put down a new carpet, and the "Curse of the Coventrys" proved the blessing of the Marches in the way of groceries and gowns.

Wealth is certainly a most desirable thing, but poverty has its sunny side, and one of the sweet uses of adversity is the genuine satisfaction which comes from hearty work of head or hand; and to the inspiration of necessity, we owe half the wise, beautiful, and useful blessings of the world. Jo enjoyed a taste of this satisfaction, and ceased to envy richer girls, taking great comfort in the knowledge that she could supply her own wants, and need ask no one for a penny.

Little notice was taken of her stories, but they found a market; and, encouraged by this fact, she resolved to make a bold stroke for fame and fortune. Having copied her novel for the fourth time, read it to all her confidential friends, and submitted it with fear and trembling to three publishers, she at last disposed of it, on condition that she would cut it down one third, and omit all the parts which she particularly admired.

"Now I must either bundle it back into my tin-kitchen to mould, pay for printing it myself, or chop it up to suit purchasers, and get what I can for it. Fame is a very good thing to have in the house, but cash is more convenient; so I wish to take the sense of the meeting on this important subject," said Jo, calling a family council.

"Don't spoil your book, my girl, for there is more in it than you know, and the idea is well worked out. Let it wait and ripen," was her father's advice; and he practiced as he preached, having waited patiently thirty years for fruit of his own to ripen, and being in no haste to gather it, even now, when it was sweet and mellow.

The dashing character of Robin Hood, the benevolent outlaw who gathered together a band of "merry men" to steal from the rich and give to the poor, has been beloved by generations. Is he based on a real, historical figure, or just the stuff of legend? We're not really sure. Louis Rhead, an Englishman writing in the early 1900's, created a compelling version of this hero. The first of the two stories collected here recounts the first meeting of Robin and one of his staunchest friends. The second tale reveals Robin in a prankish mood: Fearing himself bested by Little John for cleverness, he sets out to commit mischief on a scale large enough to prove that he is still king of the forest.

Robin Hood

RETOLD BY LOUIS RHEAD

ROBIN HOOD FIGHTS LITTLE JOHN

Robin said to his jolly bowmen, "This day I mean to fare forth to seek adventures. Mayhap I shall find some tall knight or fat abbot with an overfull purse."

Picking out a few followers, he said to the rest, "Pray, tarry, my merry men, in this our grove, and see that ye heed well my call, for should I be hard bestead I will sound three blasts on my horn, and then ye shall know that I am in dire need. So come to help me with all speed."

So saying, he wended his way with those he had chosen, to the outskirts of Sherwood Forest. At last they came to a meadow hard by a village, through which flowed a stream, little but deep.

"Bide here, my lads," quoth Robin, "behind these trees, while I go forth to meet yon tall fellow whom I see stalking forth this way."

So Robin started toward a long, narrow bridge made of a huge, flattened tree-trunk that spanned the brook. Now it chanced that both he and the stranger set foot upon the bridge at the same instant. They eyed each other up and down, and

Robin said to himself, "This tall, lusty blade would be a proper man for our band, for he stands nigh seven foot high, and hath a mighty frame." Then, to test if the fellow's valor were equal to his height, bold Robin sturdily stood and said, "Get off the bridge and give way. Dost thou not see there's no room for both to cross?"

"Get off thyself, thou saucy knave, or I'll baste thy hide with my staff," the stranger replied.

Then Robin drew from his quiver a long, straight shaft and fitted it to his bow-string.

"Thou pratest like an ass," quoth he. "Ere thou couldst strike me one blow I could send this goose-winged shaft through thy heart."

"None but a base coward would shoot at my breast while I have naught but a staff in my hand to reach thee."

At this Robin lowered his bow and thrust the shaft back into the quiver. "I scorn thee," he said, "as I do the name of a coward, and to prove that I fear thee not let me lay by my long-bow and choose a tough staff of ground-oak from yonder thicket. Then here upon this narrow bridge we will fight, and whosoever shall be doused in the brook shall own himself beaten."

The tall stranger replied, "That suits me full well to a dot, and here will I abide till thou comest."

Then bold Robin strode off to the thicket, where he cut and trimmed a trusty, knotted six-foot staff. Sooth to say, the more he looked upon the stranger the less he relished coming to blows with him, for he thought he had never seen a sturdier knave. None the less, he stepped upon the bridge and began to flourish his staff above his head right bravely. With watchful eyes and careful tread both stepped forward till they met in the middle.

In a trice, Robin gave the stranger a crack on his broad neck that made his bones ring like stones in a tin can; but he was as tough as he was big, and he said naught but, "One good turn deserves another." With that, he whirled his great staff faster and faster, bringing it down on Robin's guard with such a rain of blows that one would think twenty men were at it. Both played so rapidly and the blows were so deftly struck that neither one after half an hour's battle seemed to gain a whit. Robin tried all his skill in parrying and feinting, but he could do no more than give the stranger a whack on his ribs and shoulder which only made him grunt. As he began to grow weary the other laid on the faster, so that Robin's jacket smoked with many a thwack and he felt as if he were on fire.

At last he got a crack on the crown that caused the blood to flow down his cheek, but he only fought the more fiercely and pressed on so hard that the stranger slipped and

nigh fell over. But he regained his footing, and with a furious onslaught he brought his staff down with such tremendous force that he smashed Robin's staff into smithers and topped him with a great splash full on his back into the brook.

"Prithee, good fellow, where art thou now?" quoth the stranger.

"Good faith, in the flood," quoth Robin, "and floating along with the tide."

Thereupon he waded the stream and pulled himself up on the bank by an overhanging branch. He sat him down, wet to the skin, and laughingly cried, "My brave soul, thou hast won the bout, and I'll no longer fight with thee." So saying, he set his horn to his lips and blew a loud blast, whereat the stout yeomen came running forth from behind the trees.

"Oh, what is the matter, good master?" they cried. "Thou art as wet as a drown'd rat."

"Matter or no matter," quoth Robin, "yon tall fellow hath in fighting tumbled me into the brook."

"Seize him, comrades, for in the brook he shall likewise go to cool his hot spirit," said one.

"Nay, nay, forbear," cried Robin, "he is a stout fellow. They shall do thee no harm, my tall friend. These bowmen are my followers, with three-score-and-nine others, and if thou wilt, my jolly blade, thou shalt join us and be my good right-hand man. Three good suits of Lincoln green shalt thou have each year and a full share in all we take. We'll teach thee to shoot the fat fallow deer, and thou shalt eat sweet venison steak whene'er thou wilt, washing down with foaming ale. What saist thou, sweet chuck?"

The stranger replied, "Here is my hand on't, and with my whole heart will I serve so bold a leader, for no man living doubteth that I, John Little, can play my part with the best. But on one condition will I join your band."

"And what may that be?" quoth Robin.

"It is that ye show me an archer who can mend a shot I shall shoot with stout longbow and arrow."

"Well, thou shalt shoot," quoth Robin, "and we will mend thy shot if we may." So saying, he went and cut a willow wand about the thickness of a man's thumb and, peeling off the skin, set it up before a tree fivescore paces away. "Now," quoth he, "do thou choose a bow to thy liking from among all my men, and let us see thy skill."

"That I will, blithely," quoth John. Choosing the stoutest bow and straightest arrow he could find among a group lying on the sward, he took most careful aim, pulling the arching bow to its utmost stretch. The arrow flew, and lodged with its point right through the wand. "A brave shot!" cried the archers all.

"Canst thou mend that, bold outlaw?" asked John.

"I cannot mend the shot, but I'll notch thy shaft in twain." So saying, Robin took his bow, put on a new string, and chose a perfect, straight arrow with gray goose feathers truly tied. Then, bending the great bow, he let fly the shaft. For a moment the archers watched, breathless; then, with shouts of glee, they saw the stranger's arrow split fairly in twain.

"Enough," quoth John. "Never before have I seen so true an eye guide a shaft. Now I know an archer fit to serve."

All cried out that he had said well, and then in right merry mood they started back to their forest home, there to feast and christen their new comrade.

"What name shall we call this pretty sweet babe?"

A bald-headed yeoman, offering to act the part of priest, answered, "This infant," quoth he, "was called John Little, but that name we shall change anon. Henceforth, wherever he goes, not John Little but Little John shall he be called."

The liquor was then poured over John's head, trickling down his face; and so they baptized him. With shouts of laughter that made the forest ring, in which Little John Merrily joined, the christening came to an end with sweet song and jocund jest.

Then Robin took Little John to the treasure chamber and gave him a suit of Lincoln green and great bow of yew.

ROBIN TRIES HIS HAND SELLING MEATS

Little John had been getting the better of the Sheriff quite regularly, and, while Robin Hood owned that his right–hand man was craftier than he had thought, he resolved that he would not be outdone, but would himself show the Sheriff a thing or two. Robin and his band had no hatred against the Sheriff, nor, for that matter, against anyone else, much cause as they had to be bitter against the world, for they were all outlawed men. What they did was done in a spirit of jovial frolic and fun. It is certain that they never did any foul misdeed. They robbed the rich, who robbed others, that they might live and have means to help the poor and needy. In those cruel old days, when might seemed to make right, few were so kind and honest as Robin Hood and his merry men. Robin himself often went to mass at the little church on the outskirts of the forest, where he was welcomed because of his many lavish gifts. For he loved the humble and sincere churchmen even as he hated the purse-proud and selfish.

It fell upon a day that Robin started off alone through the forest singing a blithesome song. He had not gone far when he chanced to meet a jolly butcher, who likewise was singing merrily as he rode through the wood among the leaves so green. The butcher bestrode a fine mare, and swinging from behind on each side hung two great silk bags full of meat he was taking to Nottingham market to sell.

"Good morrow, my fine fellow," quoth jolly Robin. "Tell me what gods thou hast in thy panniers, for I have a mind for thy company and would fain know thy trade and where thou dost dwell."

"Truly, a butcher am I, and to Nottingham do I go to sell my meats. But what is it to thee where I do dwell? Tell me thy name."

"My name is Robin Hood, and in Sherwood do I dwell."

Then in a trembling voice the butcher said, "I cry your mercy, good Robin, for I fear that name. Have mercy on me and mind; let me go on my way."

"Nay, jolly butcher," quoth Robin, "fear nothing, for I will do thee no harm. Come, tell me, what is the price of thy meat and of thy mare, for, by the mass, be it never so dear, I fain would be a butcher."

"I will soon tell thee," quoth the butcher. Then he looked straight before him and for a space seemed lost in thought. At last he said, "Good Robin, I like thee well and would not offend thee. Therefore thou shalt have my meats, and eke my bonny mare, for four marks, though the price be beggarly."

"Get down from thy horse," quoth Robin, "and come, count out the money from my bag. Right gladly do I pay thy price, for I long to be a butcher for a day, and I warrant I shall sell my wares first of them all at the market."

When the butcher had seen the money counted aright he snugly packed it away in a little bag in his pouch, well content with his bargain; and Robin, mounting the horse, jogged off to Nottingham market. First of all, he got from the officers of the guild a market-stand, for which he paid a small fee. Then he put on the butcher's apron, cap, and jacket, cleaned off the stand, got out all the legs and shoulders of mutton and veal, sharpened his knives, and was soon busy with cleaver and saw, cutting up pieces to make the best display in the market.

All the other butchers looked askance at Robin because he was a stranger and seemed ignorant of the ways and sly tricks of the trade. However, when all was set out to the best advantage, he began to cry out in a loud voice, "Come hither, good people, come and buy, buy, buy. I sell good meat cheap, and cheap meat good. Pay no heed to the other butchers, for they sell naught but bone and skin. Be not backward good wives, good maids, good widows, and good spinsters; come up, come up and buy. I sell as much meat for one penny as you will get from the other butchers for three pennies. I will cut away all the fat and sell you the lean. An' it please you, good dames, I will strip away all the bones and sell naught but flesh. As for the bones, ye shall take them home to your dogs. Six pounds of good fresh meat, with never a bone, for one penny!"

So lustily did Robin cry his wares that soon a throng of dames and lasses pressed about his stand, while scarce a soul came near the booths of the other butchers. Ere long his trade was so brisk that he had no need to shout. Then, when a pretty lass asked the price of a piece of meat, he would answer, "Naught, but one kiss from thy pretty lips." Thus the handsome young butcher got many a kiss, which gladdened him more than silver coins. Long before the market closed Robin was clean sold out, and the others were full wroth because they had not thriven that day. They talked with one another, saying, "Surely he is some prodigal, that hath sold his father's land and now wastes the money in selling meat at so low a price." Said one, "Perhaps his is a man of much store and cattle. We had best be friendly with him." So several of them stepped up to Robin, saying, "Come, brother, we be all of one trade, and the Butchers' Guild is to dine with the Sheriff. Wilt thou join us in the feast?"

"Ay, marry, that will I," quoth merry Robin. "I will go with my true brethren as fast as I can hie."

So they all marched off together to the Sheriff's house. The Sheriff had been told of this wonderful butcher who could afford to sell as much meat for a penny as the others did for three pennies, so he made up his mind to place Robin beside him as the honored guest, thinking to lure the young spendthrift into some bad bargain.

While the butchers were drinking at Robin's expense they smiled and nudged one another and talked in whispers. "This is a mad blade," said one of them; "a wise one saves, and a fool spends." The Sheriff whispered to his left-hand neighbor, "His father hath left him lands which he hath sold for silver and gold, and now means to be rid of its cares." Then he said to himself, " 'Twere a good deed to help him in so worthy a purpose."

"Good fellow," quoth he to Robin, "hast thou any horned beasts to sell unto me?"

"Yea, good master Sheriff, that I have—some 200, as well a 100 acres of good land, and it please you to see it. And I will make as good a bargain of it to you as my father did make to me."

"What is the price thou askest, my good fellow, for the two hundred horned beasts? For if the price be within reason, I warrant I shall find one who will buy."

"The price to thee noble Sheriff, shall be small enough. 'Tis but 200 pounds."

"Ay," thought the Sheriff, "but one quarter of their true worth. I must go to see these same horned beasts before it chance he change his price. By my faith good fellow," he said aloud, "I fain would look upon thy 200 horned beasts."

"That is easily done," quoth Robin, "for they are not far to seek."

So when the feast was ended the Sheriff had his palfrey saddled, put 200 pounds in gold in his pouch, and made ready to go with the spendthrift butcher. Robin saddled his mare, and away they rode to the forest of merry Sherwood.

As they were passing through the leafy woods the Sheriff crossed himself, saying, "God save us this day from that naughty varlet, Robin Hood!"

"Amen, so be it," said jolly Robin, who was leading deeper and deeper into the forest.

When they had gone a little farther, bold Robin chanced to spy 100 head of good red deer that came tripping along full nigh their path. "Look you," quoth he, "how like you my horned beasts, good master Sheriff? Are they not fat and fair to see?"

Then the Sheriff was wroth and fearful. He trembled in his boots, for a sad thought of a sudden flashed through his brain. Quoth he, "I tell you, good fellow, I would I were gone from this forest, for I like not thy company nor thy fat beasts."

"Tarry but a moment, Sir Sheriff," quoth Robin, and, putting his horn to his mouth, he blew three blasts, whereat Little John and all his company came running.

"What is thy will, my good master?" cried Little John.

"I have brought hither," laughed jolly Robin, "the Sheriff of Nottingham this day to dine with three."

"Then, by Saint Swithin, he is right welcome to me, and I hope he will honestly pay for the feast, for I know he has gold. I can smell it in his pouch and I warrant if it be well counted there will be enough to serve us with wine to drink a whole year."

Then Little John lovingly grasped the Sheriff round the waist and drew him down from his palfrey. Taking his mantle gently from his back, he laid it on the ground. The proud Sheriff stood still and doleful while Robin opened his pouch and jingled out the 200 pounds in golden coins into the mantle. Little John carefully picked up the golden pieces and deftly cast the cloak again upon the Sheriff's back, then set him upon his dapple-gray palfrey, saying, "Adieu, good Sheriff, I wish thee a safe journey home."

Robin took the bridle-rein and led the palfrey to the edge of the forest, where he bade the Sheriff God-speed.

"Commend me to your lady wife at home," quoth he, "and tell her that Robin Hood found much profit in the butcher's trade in fair Nottingham town this day." So Robin went away laughing to his bower.

Rebecca—a wide-eyed, sprightly, and intelligent girl—is sent from her family's farm to live with her two strict aunts, Miranda and Jane. She brings vitality, mischief, and poetry to their household, and to the whole town, as well! Here, we witness Rebecca's effect on her schoolmate, Samuel "Seesaw" Simpson, and on her intrigued young teacher.

Rebecca of Sunnybrook Farm

KATE DOUGLAS WIGGIN

CHAPTER V
WISDOM'S WAYS

Samuel Simpson was generally called Seesaw because of his difficulty in making up his mind. Whether it were a question of fact, of spelling, or of date, of going swimming or fishing, of choosing a book in the Sunday-school library or a stick of candy at the village store, he had no sooner determined on one plan of action than his wish fondly reverted to the opposite one. Seesaw was pale, flaxen-haired, blue-eyed, round-shouldered, and given to stammering when nervous. Perhaps because of his very weakness, Rebecca's decision of character had a fascination for him, and although she snubbed him to the verge of madness, he could never keep his eyes away from her. When, having obtained permission, she walked to the water-pail in the corner and drank from the dipper, unseen forces dragged Seesaw from his seat to go and drink after her. It was not only

that there was something akin to association and intimacy in drinking next, but there was the fearful joy of meeting her in transit, and receiving a cold and disdainful look from her wonderful eyes.

On a certain warm day in summer, Rebecca's thirst exceeded the bounds of propriety. When she asked a third time for permission to quench it at the common fountain Miss Dearborn nodded yes, but lifted her eyebrows unpleasantly as Rebecca neared the desk. As she replaced the dipper Seesaw promptly raised his hand, and Miss Dearborn indicated a weary affirmative.

"What is the matter with you, Rebecca?" she asked.

"I had salt mackerel for breakfast," answered Rebecca.

There seemed nothing humorous about this reply, which was merely the statement of a fact, but an irrepressible titter ran through the school. Miss Dearborn did not enjoy jokes neither made nor understood by herself, and her face flushed.

"I think you had better stand by the pail for five minutes, Rebecca; it may help you to control your thirst."

Rebecca's heart fluttered. She had to stand in the corner by the water-pail and be stared at by all the scholars. She unconsciously made a gesture of angry dissent and moved a step nearer her seat, but was arrested by Miss Dearborn's command in a still firmer voice.

"Stand by the pail, Rebecca! Samuel, how many times have you asked for water today?"

"This is the f-f-fourth."

"Don't touch the dipper, please. The school has done nothing but drink this afternoon; it has had no time whatever to study. I suppose you had something salty for breakfast, Samuel?" queried Miss Dearborn with sarcasm.

"I had m-m-mackerel, j-just like Reb-b-becca." (Irrepressible giggles by the school.)

"I judged so. Stand by the other side of the pail, Samuel."

Rebecca's head was bowed with shame and wrath. Life looked too black a thing to be endured. The punishment was bad enough, but to be coupled in correction with Seesaw Simpson was beyond human endurance.

Singing was the last exercise in the afternoon, and Minnie Smellie chose "Shall we Gather at the River?" It was a baleful choice and seemed to hold some secret and subtle association with the situation and general progress of events; or at any rate there was apparently some obscure reason for the energy and vim with which the scholars shouted the choral invitation again and again:

Shall we gather at the river—
The beautiful, the beautiful river?

Miss Dearborn stole a look at Rebecca's bent head and was frightened.

"You may go to your seat, Rebecca," said Miss Dearborn at the end of the first song. "Samuel, stay where you are till the close of school. And let me tell you, scholars, that I asked Rebecca to stand by the pail only to break up this habit of incessant drinking, which is nothing but empty-mindedness and desire to walk to and fro over the floor. Every time Rebecca has asked for a drink today the whole school has gone to the pail one after another. She is really thirsty, and I dare say I ought to have punished you for following her example, not her for setting it. What shall we sing now, Alice?"

" 'The Old Oaken Bucket,' please."

"Think of something dry, Alice, and change the subject. Yes, 'The Star-Spangled Banner,' if you like, or anything else."

Rebecca sank into her seat and pulled the singing-book from her desk. Miss Dearborn's public explanation had shifted some of the weight from her heart, and she felt a trifle raised in her self-esteem.

Under cover of the general relaxation of singing, votive offerings of respectful sympathy began to make their appearance at her shrine. Living Perkins, who could not sing, dropped a piece of maple sugar in her lap as he passed her on his way to the blackboard to draw the map of Maine. Alice Robinson rolled a perfectly new slate pencil over the floor with her foot until it reached Rebecca's place, while her seat-mate, Emma Jane, had made up a little mound of paper balls and labelled them "Bullets for you know who."

Altogether existence grew brighter, and when she was left alone with the teacher for her grammar lesson she had nearly recovered her equanimity, which was more than Miss Dearborn had. The last clattering foot had echoed through the hall, Seesaw's backward glance of penitence had been met and answered defiantly by one of cold disdain.

"Rebecca, I am afraid I punished you more than I meant," said Miss Dearborn, who was only 18 herself, and in her year of teaching at country schools had never encountered a child like Rebecca.

"I hadn't missed a question this whole day, nor whispered either," quavered the culprit; "and I don't think I ought to be shamed just for drinking."

"You started all the others, or it seemed as if you did. Whatever you do they all do, whether you laugh, or miss, or write notes, or ask to leave the room, or drink; and it must be stopped."

"Sam Simpson is a copycat!" stormed Rebecca. "I wouldn't have minded standing in the corner alone—that is, not so very much; but I couldn't bear standing with him."

"I saw that you couldn't, and that's the reason I told you to take your seat, and left him in the corner. Remember that you are a stranger in the place, and they take notice of what you do, so you must be careful. Now let's have our conjugations. Give me the verb 'to be,' potential mood, past-perfect tense."

> *"I might have been.*
> *Thou mightst have been.*
> *He might have been.*
> *We might have been.*
> *You might have been.*
> *They might have been."*

"Give me an example, please."

> *"I might have been glad.*
> *Thou mightst have been glad.*
> *He, she, or it might have been glad."*

" 'He' or 'she' might have been glad because they are masculine and feminine, but could 'it' have been glad?" asked Miss Dearborn, who was very fond of splitting hairs.

"Why not?" asked Rebecca.

"Because 'it' is neuter gender."

"Couldn't we say, 'The kitten might have been glad if it had known it was not going to be drowned'?"

"Ye—es," Miss Dearborn answered hesitatingly, never very sure of herself under Rebecca's fire; "but though we often speak of a baby, a chicken, or a kitten as 'it,' they are really masculine or feminine gender, not neuter."

Rebecca reflected a long moment and then asked, "Is a hollyhock neuter?"

"Oh yes, of course it is, Rebecca."

"Well, couldn't we say, 'The hollyhock might have been glad to see the rain, but there was a weak little hollyhock bud growing out of its stalk, and it was afraid that there might be hurt by the storm; so the big hollyhock was kind of afraid, instead of being real glad'?"

Miss Dearborn looked puzzled as she answered, "Of course, Rebecca, hollyhocks could not be sorry, or glad, or afraid, really."

"We can't tell, I s'pose," replied the child; "but I think they are, anyway. Now what shall I say?"

"The subjunctive mood, past-perfect tense of the verb 'to know'."

"If I had known.
If thou hadst known.
If he had known.
If we had known.
If you had known.
If they had known.

"Oh, it is the saddest tense!" sighed Rebecca, with a little break in her voice; "nothing but ifs, ifs, ifs! And it makes you feel that if they had known, things might have been better!"

Miss Dearborn had not thought of it before, but on reflection she believed the subjunctive mood was a "sad" one, and "if" rather a sorry "part of speech."

"Give me some examples of the subjunctive, Rebecca, and that will do for this afternoon," she said.

"If I had not loved mackerel, I should not have been thirsty," said Rebecca with an April smile, as she closed her grammar. "If thou hadst loved me truly, thou wouldst not have stood me up in the corner. If Samuel had not loved wickedness, he would not have followed me to the water-pail."

"And if Rebecca had loved the rules of the school, she would have controlled her thirst," finished Miss Dearborn with a kiss, and the two parted friends.

The story of Heidi was written in 1880. It is about a five-year-old orphan who is brought to live with her grandfather on a remote mountain in the Swiss Alps. We now visit Heidi in the Alps soon after she joins her grandfather on his farm and they are fixing her a bed on a loft in his house.

Heidi

JOHANNA SPYRI

Let us go down then, as we both think alike," said the old man, and he followed the child down the ladder. Then he went up to the hearth, pushed the big kettle aside, and drew forward the little one that was hanging on the chain, and seating himself on the round-topped, three-legged stool before the fire, blew it up into a clear bright flame. The kettle soon began to boil, and meanwhile the old man held a large piece of cheese on a long iron fork over the fire. Heidi watched all that was going on with eager curiosity. Suddenly some new idea seemed to come into her head. Presently the grandfather got up and came to the table with a jug and the cheese, and there he saw it already tidily set.

"Ah, that's right," said the grandfather, "I am glad to see that you have some ideas of your own," and as he spoke he laid the toasted cheese on a layer of bread, "but there is still something missing."

Heidi looked at the jug that was steaming away invitingly, and ran quickly back to the cupboard. She returned with two glasses and the bowl and put them down on the table.

"Good! I see you know how to set about things; but what will you do for a seat?" The grandfather himself was sitting on the only chair in the room. Heidi flew to the hearth, and dragging the three-legged stool up to the table, sat herself down upon it.

"Well, you have managed to find a seat for yourself, I see, only a rather low one I am afraid," said the grandfather, "but you would not be tall enough to reach the table even if you sat in my chair; the first thing now, however, is to have something to eat, so come along."

With that he stood up, filled the bowl with milk, got a slice of bread, and placing it on the chair, pushed it in front of Heidi on her little three-legged stool, so that she now had a table to herself. After which he went and sat down on the corner of the table and began his own meal. Heidi lifted the bowl with both hands and drank without pause till it was empty, for the thirst of her long hot journey had returned upon her.

"Was the milk nice?" asked her grandfather.

"I never drank anything so good before," answered Heidi.

"Then you must have some more," and the old man filled her bowl again to the brim and set it before the child, who was now hungrily beginning her bread, having first spread it with the cheese, which after being toasted was soft as butter; the two together tasted

deliciously, and the child looked the picture of content as she sat eating, and at intervals taking further draughts of the milk. The meal being over, the grandfather went outside to put the goat-shed in order, and Heidi watched with interest as he first swept it out, and then put the fresh straw for goats to sleep upon. Then he went to the little well-shed and cut some long round sticks, and a small round board; in this he bored some holes and stuck the sticks into them, and there, as if by magic, there was a three-legged stool just like her grandfather's, only higher. Heidi stood and looked at it, speechless with astonishment.

"What do you think that is?" asked her grandfather.

"It's my stool, I know, because it is such a high one; and it was made all of a minute," said the child, still lost in wonder and admiration.

"She understands what she sees, her eyes are in the right place," remarked the grandfather to himself.

And so the time passed happily on till evening. Then the wind began to roar louder than ever through the old fir trees; Heidi listened with delight to the sound, and it filled her heart so full of gladness that she skipped and danced round the old trees. The grandfather stood and watched her from the shed.

Suddenly a shrill whistle was heard. Heidi paused in her dancing, and the grandfather came out. Down from the heights above the goats came springing one after another, with Peter in their midst. Heidi sprang forward with a cry of joy and rushed among the flock, greeting first one and then another of her old friends of the morning. As they neared the huts the goats stood still, and then two of their number, two beautiful slender animals, one white and one brown, ran forward to where the grandfather was standing and began licking his hands, for he was holding a little salt which he always had ready for his goats on their return home. Peter disappeared with the remainder of his flock. Heidi tenderly stroked the two goats in turn, running first to one side of them and then the other, and jumping about in her glee at the pretty little animals. "Are they ours, grandfather? Are they both ours? Are you going to put them in the shed? Will they always stay with us?"

Heidi's questions came tumbling out one after the other, so that her grandfather had only time to answer each of them with "Yes, yes." When the goats had finished licking up the salt her grandfather told her to go and fetch her bowl and the bread.

Heidi obeyed and was soon back again. The grandfather milked the white goat and filled her basin, and then breaking off a piece of bread, "Now eat your supper," he said, "and then go up to bed. Cousin Dete left another little bundle for you with a nightgown

and other small things in it, which you will find at the bottom of the cupboard if you want them. I must go and shut up the goats, so be off and sleep well."

"Good night, grandfather! Good night. What are their names, grandfather, what are their names?" she called out as she ran after his retreating figure and the goats.

"The white one is named Little Swan, and the brown one Little Bear," he answered.

"Good night, Little Swan, good night, Little Bear!" she called again at the top of her voice, for they were already inside the shed. Then she sat down on the sheet and began to eat and drink, but the wind was so strong that it almost blew her away; so she made haste and finished her supper and then went indoors and climbed up to her bed, where she was soon lying as sweetly and soundly asleep as any young princess on her couch of silk.

Not long after, and while it was still twilight, the grandfather also went to bed, for he was up every morning at sunrise, and the sun came climbing up over the mountains at a very early hour during these summer months. The wind grew so tempestuous during the night, and blew in such gusts against the walls, that the hut trembled and the old beams groaned and creaked. It came howling and wailing down the chimney like voices of those in pain, and it raged with such fury among the old fir trees that here and there a branch was snapped and fell. In the middle of the night the old man got up. "The child will be frightened," he murmured half aloud. He mounted the ladder and went and stood by the child's bed.

Outside the moon was struggling with the dark, fast-driving clouds, which at one moment left it clear and shining, and the next swept over it, and all again was dark. Just now the moonlight was falling through the round window straight on to Heidi's bed. She lay under the heavy coverlid, her cheeks rosy with sleep, her head peacefully resting on her little round arm, with a happy expression on her baby face as if dreaming of something pleasant. The old man stood looking down on the sleeping child until the moon again disappeared behind the clouds and he could see no more, then he went back to bed.

Charlotte's Web tells the story of a friendship between a spider named Charlotte and a pig named Wilbur. Wilbur is facing the fate of most farm pigs—slaughter. Charlotte, devastated by this prospect, thinks of ways to prove to everyone that Wilbur is indeed special and should not be made into bacon. Here is one of Charlotte's more inventive plans.

Charlotte's Web

E.B. WHITE

CHAPTER 13

Far into the night, while the other creatures slept, Charlotte worked on her web. First she ripped out a few of the orb lines near the center. She left the radial lines alone, as they were needed for support. As she worked, her eight legs were a great help to her. So were her teeth. She loved to weave and she was an expert at it. When she was finished ripping things out, her web looked something like this:

A spider can produce several kinds of thread. She uses a dry, tough thread for foundation lines, and she uses a sticky thread for snare lines—the ones that catch and hold insects. Charlotte decided to use her dry thread for writing the new message.

"If I write the word `Terrific' with sticky thread," she thought, "every bug that comes along will get stuck in it and spoil the effect."

"Now let's see, the first letter is T."

Charlotte climbed to a point at the top of the left-hand side of the web. Swinging her spinnerets into position, she attached her thread and then dropped down. As she dropped, her spinning tubes went into action and she let out thread. At the bottom, she attached the thread. This formed the upright part of the letter T. Charlotte was not satisfied, however. She climbed up and made another attachment, right next to the first. Then she carried the line down, so that she had a double line instead of a single line. "It will show up better if I make the whole thing with double lines."

She climbed back up, moved over about an inch to the left, touched her spinnerets to the web, and then carried a line across to the right, forming the top of the T. She repeated this, making it double. Her eight legs were very busy helping.

"Now for the E!"

Charlotte got so interested in her work, she began to talk to herself, as though to cheer herself on. If you had been sitting quietly in the barn cellar that evening, you would have heard something like this:

"Now for the R! Up we go! Attach! Descend! Pay out line! Whoa! Attach! Good! Up you go! Repeat! O.K.! Easy, keep those lines together! Now, then, out and down for the leg of the R! Pay out line! Whoa! Attach! Ascend! Repeat! Good girl!"

And so, talking to herself, the spider worked at her difficult task. When it was completed, she felt hungry. She ate a small bug that she had been saving. Then she slept.

Next morning, Wilbur arose and stood beneath the web. He breathed the morning air into his lungs. Drops of dew, catching the sun, made the web stand out clearly. When Lurvy arrived with breakfast, there was the handsome pig, and over him, woven neatly in block letters, was the word TERRIFIC. Another miracle.

Lurvy rushed and called Mr. Zuckerman. Mr. Zuckerman rushed and called Mrs. Zuckerman. Mrs. Zuckerman ran to the phone and called the Arables. The Arables climbed into their truck and hurried over. Everybody stood at the pigpen and stared at the web and read the word, over and over, while Wilbur, who really felt terrific, stood quietly swelling out his chest and swinging his snout from side to side.

"Terrific!" breathed Zuckerman in joyful admiration. "Edith, you better phone the reporter on the *Weekly Chronicle* and tell him what has happened. He will want to know about this. He may want to bring a photographer. There isn't a pig in the whole state that is as terrific as our pig."

The news spread. People who had journeyed to see Wilbur when he was "some pig" came back again to see him now that he was "terrific."

That afternoon, when Mr. Zuckerman went to milk the cows and clean out the tie-ups, he was still thinking about what a wonderous pig he owned.

"Lurvy!" he called. "There is to be no more cow manure thrown down into that pig-pen. I have a terrific pig. I want that pig to have clean, bright straw every day for his bedding. Understand?"

"Yes, sir," said Lurvy.

"Furthermore," said Mr. Zuckerman, "I want you to start building a crate for Wilbur. I have decided to take the pig to the County Fair on September sixth. Make the crate large and paint it green with gold letters!"

"What will the letters say?" asked Lurvy.

"They should say Zuckerman's Famous Pig."

Lurvy picked up a pitchfork and walked away to get some clean straw. Having such an important pig was going to mean plenty of extra work, he could see that.

Below the apple orchard, at the end of a path, was the dump where Mr. Zuckerman threw all sorts of trash and stuff that nobody wanted any more. Here, in a small clearing hidden by young alders and wild raspberry bushes, was an astonishing pile of old bottles and empty tin cans and dirty rags and bits of metal and broken bottles and broken hinges and broken springs and dead batteries and last month's magazines and old discarded dishmops and tattered overalls and rusty spikes and leaky pails and forgotten stoppers and useless junk of all kinds, including a wrong-size crank for a broken ice-cream freezer.

Templeton knew the dump and liked it. There were good hiding places there—excellent cover for a rat. And there was usually a tin can with food still clinging to the inside.

Templeton was down there now, rummaging around. When he returned to the barn, he carried in his mouth an advertisement he had torn from a crumpled magazine.

"How's this?" he asked, showing the ad to Charlotte. "It says `Crunchy.' Crunchy would

be a good word to write in your web."

"Just the wrong idea," replied Charlotte. "Couldn't be worse. We don't want Zucker-man to think Wilbur is crunchy. He might start thinking about crisp crunchy bacon and tasty ham. That would put ideas into his head. We must advertise Wilbur's noble quali-ties, not his tastiness. Go get another word, please, Templeton."

The rat looked disgusted. But he sneaked away to the dump and was back in a while with a strip of cotton cloth. "How's this?" he asked. "It's a label off an old shirt."

Charlotte examined the label. It said PRE-SHRUNK.

"I'm sorry, Templeton," she said "but Pre-shrunk is out of the question. We want Zuckerman to think Wilbur is nicely filled out, not all shrunk up. I'll have to ask you to try again."

"What do you think I am, a messenger boy?" grumbled the rat. "I'm not going to spend all my time chasing down to the dump after advertising material."

"Just once more—please!" said Charlotte.

"I'll tell you what I'll do," said Templeton. "I know where there's a package of soap flakes in the woodshed. It has writing on it. I'll bring you a piece of the package."

He climbed the rope that hung on the wall and disappeared through a hole in the ceiling. When he came back he had a strip of blue-and-white cardboard in his teeth.

"There!" he said, triumphantly. "How's that?"

Charlotte read the words: "With New Radiant Action."

"What does it mean?" asked Charlotte, who had never used any soap flakes in her life.

"How should I know?" said Templeton. "You asked for words and I brought them. I suppose the next thing you'll want me to fetch is a dictionary."

Together they studied the soap ad. " 'With new radiant action,' " repeated Charlotte, slowly. "Wilbur!" she called.

Wilbur who was asleep in the straw, jumped up.

"Run around!" commanded Charlotte. "I want to see you in action, to see if you are radiant."

Wilbur raced to the end of his yard.

"Now back again, faster!" said Charlotte.

Wilbur jumped as high as he could.

"Keep your knees straight and touch the ground with your ears!" called Charlotte.

Wilbur obeyed.

"Do a back flip with a half twist in it!" cried Charlotte.

Wilbur went over backwards, writhing and twisting as he went.

"O.K., Wilbur," said Charlotte. "You can go back to sleep. O.K., Templeton, the soap ad will do, I guess. I'm not sure Wilbur's action is exactly radiant, but it's interesting."

"Actually," said Wilbur, "I feel radiant."

"Do you?" said Charlotte, looking at him with affection. "Well, you're a good little pig, and radiant you shall be. I'm in this thing pretty deep now—I might as well go the limit."

Tired from his romp, Wilbur lay down in the clean straw. He closed his eyes. The straw seemed scratchy—not as comfortable as the cow manure. Wilbur sighed. It had been a busy day—his first day of being terrific. Dozens of people had visited his yard during the afternoon, and he had to stand and pose, looking as terrific as he could. Now he was tired. Fern had arrived and seated herself quietly on her stool in the corner.

"Tell me a story, Charlotte!" said Wilbur, as he lay waiting for sleep to come. "Tell me a story!"

So Charlotte, although she, too, was tired, did what Wilbur wanted.

"Once upon a time," she began, "I had a beautiful cousin who managed to build her web across a small stream. One day a tiny fish leaped into the air and got tangled in the web. My cousin was very much surprised, of course. The fish was thrashing wildly. My cousin hardly dared tackle it. But she did. She swooped down and threw great masses of wrapping material around the fish and fought bravely to capture it."

"Did she succeed?" asked Wilbur.

"It was a never-to-be-forgotten battle," said Charlotte. "There was the fish, caught only by one fin, its tail wildly thrashing and shining in the sun. There was the web, sagging dangerously under the weight of the fish."

"How much did the fish weigh?" asked Wilbur eagerly.

"I don't know," said Charlotte. "There was my cousin, slipping in, dodging out, beaten mercilessly over the head by the wildly thrashing fish, dancing in, dancing out, throwing her threads and fighting hard. First she threw a left around the tail. The fish lashed back. Then a left to the tail and a right, and another right to the fin. Then a hard left to the head, while the web swayed and stretched."

"Then what happened?" asked Wilbur.

"Nothing," said Charlotte. "The fish lost the fight. My cousin wrapped it up so tight it couldn't budge."

"Then what happened?" asked Wilbur.

"Nothing," said Charlotte. "My cousin kept the fish for a while, and then when she got good and ready, she ate it."

"Tell me another story!" begged Wilbur.

So Charlotte told him about another cousin of hers who was an aeronaut.

"What is an aeronaut?" asked Wilbur.

"A balloonist," said Charlotte. "My cousin used to stand on her head and let out enough thread to form a balloon. Then she'd let go and be lifted into the air and carried upward on the warm wind."

"Is that true?" asked Wilbur. "Or are you just making it up?"

"It's true," replied Charlotte. "I have some very remarkable cousins. And now, Wilbur, it's time you went to sleep."

"Sing something!" begged Wilbur, closing his eyes.

So Charlotte sang a lullaby, while crickets chirped in the grass and the barn grew dark.

This was the song she sang.

> *"Sleep, sleep, my love, my only,*
> *Deep, deep, in the dung and the dark;*
> *Be not afraid and be not lonely!*
> *This is the hour when frogs and thrushes*
> *Praise the world from the woods and the rushes.*
> *Rest from care, my one and only,*
> *Deep in the dung and the dark!"*

But Wilbur was already asleep. When the song ended, Fern got up and went home.

Tales of Beatrix Potter

BEATRIX POTTER

THE TALE OF PETER RABBIT

Once upon a time there were four little Rabbits, and their names were Flopsy, Mopsy, Cotton-tail, and Peter. They lived with their Mother in a sand-bank, underneath the root of a very big fir-tree.

"Now, my dears," said old Mrs. Rabbit one morning, "you may go into the fields or down the lane, but don't go into Mr. McGregor's garden; your Father had an accident there; he was put in a pie by Mrs. McGregor. Now run along, and don't get into mischief. I am going out."

Then old Mrs. Rabbit took a basket and her umbrella, and went through the wood to the baker's. She bought a loaf of brown bread and five currant buns. Flopsy, Mopsy, and Cottontail, who were good little bunnies, went down the lane to gather blackberries. But Peter, who was very naughty, ran straight away to Mr. McGregor's garden, and squeezed under the gate!

First he ate some lettuces and some French beans; and then he ate some radishes; and then, feeling rather sick, he went to look for some parsley. But round the end of a cucumber frame, whom should he meet but Mr. McGregor's!

Mr. McGregor was on his hands and knees planting out young cabbages, but he jumped up and ran after Peter, waving a rake and calling out, "Stop thief!"

Peter was most dreadfully frightened; he rushed all over the garden, for he had forgotten the way back to the gate. He lost one of his shoes among the cabbages, and the other shoe amongst the potatoes.

After losing them, he ran on four legs and went faster, so that I think he might have got away altogether if he had not unfortunately run into a gooseberry net, and got caught by the large buttons on his jacket. It was a blue jacket with brass buttons, quite new.

Peter gave himself up for lost, and shed big tears; but his sobs were overhead by some friendly sparrows, who flew to him in great excitement, and implored him to exert himself.

Mr. McGregor came up with a sieve, which he intended to pop upon the top of Peter; but Peter wriggled out just in time, leaving his jacket behind. And rushed into the toolshed, and jumped into a can. It would have been a beautiful thing to hide in, if it had not had so much water in it.

Mr. McGregor was quite sure that Peter, was somewhere in the toolshed, perhaps hidden underneath a flower-pot. He began to turn them over carefully, looking under each. Presently Peter sneezed—"Kertyschoo!" Mr. McGregor was after him in no time, and tried to put his foot upon Peter, who jumped out of a window, upsetting three plants. The window was too small for Mr. McGregor, and he was tired of running after Peter. He went back to his work.

Peter sat down to rest; he was out of breath and trembling with fright, and he had not the least idea which way to go. Also he was very damp with sitting in that can. After a time he began to wander about, going lippity—lippity—not very fast, and looking all around. He found a door in a wall; but it was locked, and there was no room for a fat little rabbit to squeeze underneath. An old mouse was running in and out over the stone doorstep, carrying peas and beans to her family in the wood. Peter asked her the way to the gate, but she had such a large pea in her mouth that she could not answer. She only shook her head at him. Peter began to cry.

He went back towards the toolshed, but suddenly quite close to him, he heard the noise of a hoe—scratch, scratch, scritch. Peter scuttered underneath the bushes. But presently, as nothing happened, he came out, and climbed upon a wheelbarrow, and peeped over. The first thing he saw was Mr. McGregor hoeing onions. His back was turned towards

Peter, and beyond him was the gate! Peter got down very quietly off the wheelbarrow, and started running as fast as he could go, along a straight walk behind some black-currant bushes.

Mr. McGregor caught sight of him at the corner, but Peter did not care. He slipped underneath the gate, and was safe at last in the wood outside the garden. Mr. McGregor hung up the little jacket and the shoes for a scare-crow to frighten the blackbirds.

Peter never stopped running or looked behind him till he got home to the big fir-tree. He was so tired that he flopped down upon the nice soft sand on the floor of the rabbit-hole, and shut his eyes. His mother was busy cooking; she wondered

what he had done with his clothes. It was the second little jacket and pair of shoes that Peter had lost in a fortnight!

I am sorry to say that Peter was not very well during the evening. His mother put him to bed, and made some camomile tea; and she gave a dose of it to Peter!

"One tablespoonful to be taken at bedtime!"

But Flopsy, Mopsy, and Cotton-tail had bread and milk and blackberries for supper.

THE TALE OF THE FLOPSY BUNNIES

It is said that the effect of eating too much lettuce is "soporific." I have never felt sleepy after eating lettuces; but then I am not a rabbit. They certainly had a very soporific effect upon the Flopsy Bunnies!

When Benjamin Bunny grew up, he married his cousin Flopsy. They had a large family, and they were very improvident and cheerful. I do not remember the separate names of their children; they were generally called the "Flopsy Bunnies." As there was not always quite enough to eat— Benjamin used to borrow cabbages from

Flopsy's brother, Peter Rabbit, who kept a nursery garden. Sometimes Peter Rabbit had no cabbages to spare. When this happened, the Flopsy Bunnies went across the field to a rubbish heap, in the ditch outside Mr. McGregor's garden.

Mr. McGregor's rubbish heap was a mixture. There were jam pots and paper bags, and mountains of chopped grass from the mowing machine (which always tasted oily), and some rotten vegetable marrows and an old boot or two. One day—oh joy!—there were a quantity of overgrown lettuces, which had "shot" into flower. The Flopsy Bunnies simply stuffed lettuces. By degrees, one after another, they were overcome with slumber, and lay down in the mown grass.

Benjamin was not so much overcome as his children. Before going to sleep he was sufficiently wide awake to put a paper bag over his head to keep off the flies. The little Flopsy Bunnies slept delightfully in the warm sun. From the lawn beyond the garden came the distant clacketty sound of the mowing machine. The blue-bottles buzzed about the wall, and a little old mouse picked over the rubbish among the jam pots. (I can tell you her name, she was called Thomasina Tittlemouse, a woodmouse with a long tail.) She rustled across the paper bag, and awakened Benjamin Bunny. The mouse apologized profusely, and said that she knew Peter Rabbit.

While she and Benjamin were talking, close under the wall, they heard a heavy tread above their heads; and suddenly Mr. McGregor emptied out a sackful of lawn mowings right upon the sack of sleeping Flopsy Bunnies! Benjamin shrank down under his paper bag. The mouse hid in the jam pot.

The little rabbits smiled sweetly in their sleep under the shower of grass; they did not awake because the lettuces had been so soporific. They dreamt that their mother Flopsy was tucking them up in a hay bed.

Mr. McGregor looked down after emptying his sack. He saw some funny little brown tips of ears sticking up thorough the lawn mowings. He stared at them for some time. Presently a fly settled on one of them and it moved. Mr. McGregor climbed down on to the rubbish heap—

"One, two, three, four! five! six leetle rabbits!" said he as he dropped them into his

sack. The Flopsy Bunnies dreamt that their mother was turning them over in bed. They stirred a little in their sleep, but still they did not wake up. Mr. McGregor tied the sack and left it on the wall. He went to put away the mowing machine.

While he was gone, Mrs. Flopsy Bunny (who had remained at home) came across the field. She looked suspiciously at the sack and wondered where everybody was. Then the mouse came out of her jam pot, and Benjamin took the paper bag off his head, and they told the doleful tale. Benjamin and Flopsy were in despair, they could not undo the string. But Mrs. Tittlemouse was a resourceful person. She nibbled a hole in the bottom corner of the sack.

The little rabbits were pulled out and pinched to wake them. Their parents stuffed the empty sack with three rotten vegetable marrows, an old blacking brush and two decayed turnips.

Then they all hid under a bush and watched for Mr. McGregor. Mr. McGregor came back and picked up the sack, and carried it off. He carried it hanging down, as if it were rather heavy. The Flopsy Bunnies followed at a safe distance. They watched him go into his house. And then they crept up to the window to listen.

Mr. McGregor threw down the sack on the floor in a way that would have been extremely painful to the Flopsy Bunnies, if they had happened to have been inside it.

They could hear him drag his chair on the flags, and chuckle—

"One, two, three, four, five, six leetle rabbits!" said Mr. McGregor.

"Eh? What's that? What have they been spoiling now?" enquired Mrs. McGregor.

"One, two, three, four, five, six leetle fat rabbits!" repeated Mr. McGregor, counting on his fingers—"One, two, three—"

"Don't you be silly: What do you mean, you silly old man?"

"In the sack! One, two, three, four, five, six!" replied Mr. McGregor.

(The youngest Flopsy Bunny got upon the windowsill.)

Mrs. McGregor took hold of the sack and felt it. She said she could feel six, but they must be old rabbits, because they were so hard and all different shapes.

"Not fit to eat; but the skins will do fine to line my old cloak."

"Line your old cloak?" shouted Mr. McGregor—"I shall sell them to buy myself baccy!"

"Rabbit tobacco! I shall skin them and cut off their heads."

Mrs. McGregor untied the sack and put her hand inside. When she felt the vegetables she became very very angry. She said that Mr. McGregor had "done it a purpose." And Mr. McGregor was very angry too. One of the rotten marrows came flying through the kitchen window, and hit the youngest Flopsy Bunny. It rather hurt. Then Benjamin and Flopsy thought that it was time to go home. So Mr. McGregor did not get his tobacco, and Mrs. McGregor did not get her rabbit skins.

But next Christmas Thomasina Tittlemouse got a present of enough rabbit wool to make herself a cloak and a hood, and a handsome muff and a pair of warm mittens.

THE TALE OF TOM KITTEN

Once upon a time there were three little kittens, and their names were Mittens, Tom Kitten, and Moppet. They had dear little fur coats of their own; and they tumbled about the doorstep and played in the dust.

But one day their mother—Mrs. Tabitha Twitchet—expected friends to tea; so she

fetched the kittens indoors, to wash and dress them, before the fine company arrived. First she scrubbed their faces. Then she brushed their fur. Then she combed their tails and whiskers. Tom was very naughty, and he scratched.

Mrs. Tabitha dressed Moppet and Mittens in clean pinafores and tuckers; and then she took all sorts of elegant uncomfortable clothes out of a chest of drawers, in order to dress up her son Thomas. Tom Kitten was very fat, and he had grown; several buttons burst off. His mother sewed them on again.

When the three kittens were ready, Mrs. Tabitha unwisely turned them out into the garden, to be out of the way while she made hot buttered toast.

"Now keep your frocks clean, children! You must walk on your hind legs. Keep away from the dirty ash-pit, and from Sally Henny Penny, and from the pigsty and the Puddle-ducks."

Moppet and Mittens walked down the garden path unsteadily. Presently they trod upon their pinafores and fell on their noses. When they stood up there were several green smears!

"Let us climb up the rockery and sit on the garden wall," said Moppet.

They turned their pinafores back to front and went up with a skip and a jump; Moppet's white tucker fell down into the road. Tom Kitten was quite unable to jump when walking upon his hind legs in his trousers. He came up the rockery by degrees, breaking the ferns and shedding buttons right and left. He was all in pieces when he reached the top of the wall.

Moppet and Mittens tried to pull him together; his hat fell off, and the rest of his buttons burst. While they were in difficulties, there was a pit pat, paddle pat! and the three Puddle-ducks came along the hard high road, marching one behind the other and doing the goose step—pit, pat, paddle pat! pit pat, waddle pat!

They stopped and stood in a row and stared up at the kittens. They had very small eyes and looked surprised. The two duck-birds, Rebeccah and Jemima Puddle-duck, picked up the hat and tucker and put them on.

Mittens laughed so that she fell off the wall. Moppet and Tom descended after her; the pinafores and all the rest of Tom's clothes came off on the way down.

"Come! Mr. Drake Puddle-duck," said Moppet. "Come and help us dress him! Come button up Tom!"

Mr. Drake Puddle-duck advanced in a slow sideways manner and picked up the various

articles. But he put them on himself! They fitted him even worse than Tom Kitten.

"It's a very fine morning!" said Mr. Drake Puddle-duck.

And he and Jemima and Rebeccah Puddle-duck set off up the road, keeping step—pit pat, paddle pat! pit pat, waddle pat! Then Tabitha Twitchet came down to the garden and found her kittens on the wall with no clothes on. She pulled them off the wall, smacked them, and took them back to the house.

"My friends will arrive in a minute, and you are not fit to be seen; I am affronted," said Mrs. Tabitha Twitchet.

She sent them upstairs; and I am sorry

to say she told her friends that they were in bed with the measles—which was not true. Quite the contrary; they were not in bed: not in the least.

Somehow there were very extraordinary noises overhead, which disturbed the dignity and repose of the tea party. And I think that some day I shall have to make another, larger book, to tell you more about Tom Kitten!

As for the Puddle-ducks—they went into a pond. The clothes all came off directly, because there were no buttons. And Mr. Drake Puddle-duck, and Jemima and Rebeccah, have been looking for them ever since.

Bibliography

Alcott, Louisa May. *Little Women*. New York: Barnes & Noble Books, 1994.

Andersen, Hans C. *Andersen's Fairy Tales*. Illustrated by Troy Howell. Stamford: Longmeadow Press, 1988.
Other Editions:
—. *Andersen's Fairy Tales: Classic Fairy Tales.* New York: Crown Publishers, 1989.
—. *Complete Hans Christian Andersen Fairy Tales.* New York: Random House. 1993.

Barrie, J.M. *Peter Pan.* New York: Dell Yearling, 1985.
Other Editions:
—. *Peter Pan.* New York: Henry Holt & Co., 1987.
—. *Peter Pan.* New York: Penguin, Puffin Books, 1993.
—. *Peter Pan: The Complete Book.* New York: Tundra Books, 1988.

Baum, L. Frank. *The Wizard of Oz.* New York: Books of Wonder, 1987.
Other Editions:
—. *The Wizard of Oz.* New York: Scholastic, 1993.
—. *The Wizard of Oz.* New York: Putnam (Illustrated Junior Library) 1994.

Carroll, Lewis. *Alice in Wonderland.* New York: Dell, 1992.
Other Editions:
— *Alice In Wonderland.* New York: Norton, 1992.

Dahl Road. *Charlie and the Chocolate Factory.* New York: Penguin, Puffin Books, 1973.
Other Editions:
—. *Charlie and the Chocolate Factory.* New York: Buccaneer Books, 1992.
—. *Charlie and the Chocolate Factory.* New York: Penguin, Puffin Books, 1988.

Grimm, Jacob and Grimm, Wilhelm K. *Sleeping Beauty*. New York: Silver, 1985.
Other Editions:
Poole, Josephine, ed. *Sleeping Beauty.* New York: Barron, 1989.

Jacobs, Joseph, ed. *English Fairytales.* New York: Knopf, 1993.

Kingsley, Charles. *The Water-Babies.* New York: Oxford University Press, 1995.

Kipling, Rudyard. *Rudyard Kipling Illustrated.* New York: Crown Publishers, 1982.
Other Editions:
—. *Just So Stories.* (Illustrated); New York: Viking, 1993.
—. *Collected Stories of Rudyard Kipling.* New York: Knopf, 1994.
—. *The Best Fiction of Rudyard Kipling.* New York; Doubleday, 1989.
—. *The Jungle Book & Just So Stories.* New York: Bantam, 1986.

Lang, Andrew. *The Arabian Nights Entertainments.* New York: Dover Publications, Inc., 1969.
Other Editions:
Twain, Mark. *Arabian Nights.* New York: Putnam, 1981.
Wiggins, Kate D., and Smith, Nora A., eds. *Arabian Nights: Their Best-Known Tales.* New York: Macmillan, Macmillan Children's Group (Scribner's Young Readers), 1993.

L'Engle, Madeleine. *A Wrinkle in Time.* New York: Dell Yearling, 1973.

Lofting, Hugh. *Doctor Dolittle.* New York: Dell, 1988.

London, Jack. *The Call of the Wild.* New York: Portland House Illustrated Classics, 1987. Other Editions:
—. *Call of the Wild, White Fang & Other Stories.* ed. by Andrew Sinclair, New York: Oxford University Press, 1990.
—. *Call of the Wild & Other Stories.* New York: Silver, 1985.

McCloskey, Robert. *Homer Price.* New York: Penguin, Puffin Books, 1976.

Perrault, Charles. *Cinderella: Fairy Tales and Other Tales from Perrault*. New York: Henry Holt, 1989.
Other Editions:
Grimm, Jacob and Grimm, Wilhelm K. *Cinderella* New York: William Morrow & Co., 1981.

Potter, Beatrix. *Peter Rabbit*. New York: Random House, 1984.
Other Editions:
—. *Peter Rabbit and Eleven Other Favorite Tales*. Adapted by Pat Stewart. New York: Dover, 1994.

Robin Hood. Retold by Louis Rhead. New York: Random House, 1988.
Other Editions:
Ingle, Annie., ed. *Robin Hood*. New York: Random House, Random Books Young Readers, 1993.
Creswick, Paul., *Robin Hood*. New York: Macmillan, Macmillan Children's Group, 1984.

Sewell, Anna. *Black Beauty*. New York: Crown Publisher, 1982.
Other Editions:
—. *Black Beauty*. New York: Knopf, 1993.
—. *Black Beauty*. New York: Scholastic, 1994.
Owens, L., *Black Beauty & Other Horse Stories*. New York: Crown Publishers, 1983.

Spyri, Johanna. *Heidi*. Stamford: Longmeadow Press, 1986.

White, E.B. *Charlotte's Web*. New York: HarperCollins, Harper Trophy, 1980.
Other Editions:
—. *Charlotte's Web*. New York: HarperCollins, Harper Perennial Books, 1990.

Wiggin, Kate Douglas. *Rebecca of Sunnybrook Farm*. New York: Signet Classic, 1991.

Acknowledgments

"The Doughnuts", from HOMER PRICE by Robert McCloskey, copyright 1943, renewed (c) 1971 by Robert McCloskey. Used by permission of Viking Penguin, an imprint of Penguin Putnam Books for Young Readers, a division of Penguin Putnam Inc. All rights reserved.

Excerpt from THE LITTLE PRINCE by Antoine de Saint-Exupery, copyright 1943 and renewed 1971 by Harcourt, Inc., reprinted by permission of the publisher.
Illustrations from pages 5, 58, 59 and 62 in THE LITTLE PRINCE by Antoine de Saint-Exupery, copyright 1943 and renewed 1971 by Harcourt, Inc., reprinted by permission of the publisher.

From CHARLIE AND THE CHOCOLATE FACTORY by Roald Dahl, illustrations by Joseph Schindelman. Text and illustrations copyright (c) 1964, renewed 1992 by Roald Dahl Nominee Limited. Used by permission of Alfred A. Knopf, an imprint of Random House Children's Books, a division of Random House, Inc.

Excerpt from "The Black Thing" from A WRINKLE IN TIME by Madeleine L'Engle. Copyright 1962, renewed 1990 by Madeleine L'Engle Franklin. Reprinted by permission of Farrar, Straus and Giroux, LLC.

Copyright 1952 by E.B. White, renewed (c) 1980 by E. B. White.
Illustrations copyright (c) 1952 by Garth Williams, renewed (c) 1980 by Garth Williams. Used by permission of HarperCollins Publishers.

List of Illustrators

Mabel Lucie Attwell
Peter Pan

John Batten
Jack and the Beanstalk

Paul Bransom
The Call of the Wild

W.W. Denslow
The Wonderful Wizard of Oz

Edmund Dulac
The Tales of the Arabian Nights
Cinderella

Joseph M. Gleeson
Just So Stories

Lucy Kemp-Welch
Black Beauty

Rudyard Kipling
Just So Stories

Hugh Lofting
The Story of Doctor Dolittle

Robert McCloskey
Homer Price

Louis Rhead
Robin Hood

William Heath Robinson
Cinderella

Antoine de Saint-Exupéry
The Little Prince

Joseph Schindelman
Charlie and the Chocolate Factory

Jessie Willcox Smith
Hansel and Gretel
Heidi
Jack and the Beanstalk
Little Women
The Water Babies

Sir John Tenniel
Alice in Wonderland

Garth Williams
Charlotte's Web